Frankie's Heart

Frankie's Heart

M. Jean Pike

Black Lyon Publishing, LLC

Our books may be ordered through your local bookstore or by visiting the publisher:

www.BlackLyonPublishing.com

Black Lyon Publishing, LLC
PO Box 567
Baker City, OR 97814

This is a work of fiction. All of the characters, names, events, organizations and conversations in this novel are either the products of the author's vivid imagination or are used in a fictitious way for the purposes of this story.

ISBN-10:   1-934912-84-0
ISBN-13:   978-1-934912-84-3
Library of Congress Control Number: 2018907642

Published and printed in
the United States of America.

Black Lyon
Inspirational Romance

For Jesus Christ, my Savior, my Friend.
And for Judy Jerome, who's got a Frankie Heart.

Part One
Running Ahead of God

Chapter One

Alonzo Bonetti had been dead for exactly two hundred days when his widow, Frankie, bought the fixer-upper on Cottage Street. Unloved and unappreciated, the house spoke to Frankie's heart, asking for a second chance. And Frankie's heart said yes.

The first week, she scrubbed the house from top to bottom. She switched out the hardware on the kitchen cabinets and replaced all of the plastic switch plates with brushed nickel, things she could easily do herself. On day two hundred and ten she finished painting the living room. Hugging herself, she stood back to admire her handiwork.

The colors she'd chosen, Gray Frost walls offset by Shimmering Pearl trim, had transformed the boring beige room into a space that was soothing and sophisticated. The project had taken most of three days and all of two gallons and the end result was fabulous.

She hugged herself tighter. "I love this."

A knock at the door brought her down to earth. It couldn't be four o'clock already, could it? She'd meant to quit early and tidy herself up a bit before the contractor arrived. As usual, she'd lost track of time. She knew she was a mess, but there was no help for that now. Hooking her dark hair behind her ears, she wiped her paint-spattered hands on her jeans and went to answer the door.

The fifty-something man who stood on her porch was startlingly attractive. Somehow she hadn't expected that. Rugged, a bit ragged, with his salt and pepper hair dipping just below the neckline of his shirt, a good month overdue for a haircut. An early five o'clock shadow was already blooming into a beard on his cleft chin. Her glance skimmed over his jeans and work boots, and back to the fine lines at the corners of his incredibly blue eyes, and she regretted that she hadn't taken the time to make herself presentable.

"Are you Francesca?" he asked.

"Call me Frankie."

"Hi, Frankie. I'm Tracy Johanson. I hope Rhoda remembered to tell you I'd be stopping by today."

"Yes, she mentioned it. Please come in."

He stepped inside, his glance sweeping over her empty paint cans and brushes and the garbage bags she'd put down for drop cloths.

"Sorry about the mess. I've been painting. I'll have to do every room eventually, but one step at a time, right? At some point I want to rip out this carpet and put in hardwood floors." She was babbling. Why was she always so awkward with strangers? Why did she feel the need to fill every inch of silence with words?

"Rho said you wanted some estimates on a few jobs?"

"Yes. Yes, I do."

"Okay. Do you need a quote on the flooring?"

"Oh, no. That will be a long time down the road. There's work needed in just about every room, but I'll show you the main things."

She led him into the kitchen and pointed at the window above the sink. "I definitely can't live with that. As you can see, it's the only window in the room, and it's so cloudy I can't even see out it."

"It's got a bad seal." He pulled a tape measure from his back pocket and measured the window, then jotted a note in the pad he'd brought.

"That shouldn't be a big deal, should it? Rhoda didn't think so."

"It depends on what kind of shape the casings are in. These old houses, once you start taking them apart, you never know what you're going to run into."

She liked the way he looked in her kitchen. The way he filled the space without swallowing it up. He looked like the kind of man who appreciated a good, home-cooked meal.

"I'll go outside and take a look at the casing before I leave." Off the kitchen, she showed him the crumbling ceiling in the laundry room. "Do you see how stained this is? They put on a metal roof before they put the house up for sale, but obviously the roof leaked in here."

"For quite a long time, from the looks of it." He measured the ceiling's length and width and made a few more notes in his pad. "Do you want dry wall, or another dropped ceiling?"

"I guess I want whatever's the most affordable."

"Okay."

"This will probably be expensive to fix, won't it?"

"Again, it'll depend on what I run into once I take this old ceiling down."

She made a tour of the house, showing him the leaky bath tub, its faucet with a jammed diverter lever, and the wobbly railing on the staircase that led to her loft bedroom.

"My biggest worry is in the cellar, though," she told him.

He followed her down the rickety staircase and she indicated the floor jacks that were randomly spaced throughout the cellar. "Some of these look kind of rusty. I'm worried they might give out."

He dropped to a squat and inspected one of the jacks. "It wouldn't hurt to replace them, but I don't think there's any immediate danger."

A wave of relief washed over her and she smiled. "That's good. I'd sure hate to be sitting in my living room some evening and end up in the cellar." She let out a short, nervous bark of laughter.

He stood, his gaze traveling upward. Reaching up, he touched one of the enormous beams that spanned the length of the ceiling. "These are hand hewn beams."

"Is that good?"

"You don't see these very often anymore. People used them back in the day to build their barns and houses, because they last forever. It's a lost art form, now. They're too labor intensive." He walked the length of the cellar, his gaze trained on the ceiling. "You've got hardwood, by the way."

"What?"

"You said you wanted to put in hardwood floors. You've already got them. See?" She followed his gaze, noticing the wide planks for the first time. "No telling what kind of shape they're in, under that carpeting, but I'm sure you could have them refinished."

She grinned, delighted. "I guess I'll have to rip out the carpet and find out."

He inspected the foundation walls, the galvanized pipes, and the electric box. "This house definitely needs some work, but it's got good bones."

"That's the same exact thing my realtor said."

For the first time, he smiled. He had a lovely smile, it reached up to his eyes and made them sparkle. "Rhodie's been hanging out with me too long. She actually tried to get me to look at this house, thought I'd want to buy it for a rental property." He shrugged. "I've already got my hands full, though."

Rhodie? She thought of Rhoda Swanson, the stylish, self-assured woman who'd sold her the house. A woman who she was sure would never answer the door with paint-splashed jeans and messy hair. "You must know her pretty well."

"She's my sister."

"Oh." Why hadn't Rhoda mentioned that?

"Is there anything else you want me to look at?"

"No, I think what I've already shown you is more than enough to start with."

Back in the living room, Tracy stowed his notepad in the pocket of his tee shirt. "Some of the projects are minor. Some will involve more labor. And more cost."

"I'm on a budget, so I have to prioritize. Where would you recommend I start?"

"If it was my house, I'd start with the porch."

The porch? That wasn't even on her long-term list. "What's wrong with the porch?"

"For starters, your posts are rotted."

She sighed. Her budget was pretty small. Rebuilding the porch would likely take half of the money she'd earmarked for repairs. If she did that, Lord knew how many other projects wouldn't get done.

"I really hadn't planned on redoing the porch just yet."

"Well, you'd better plan on it, if you want to keep it. It's not safe to sit on as it is. Those rotting posts aren't going to support the weight of the roof much longer."

His gruff tone surprised her. It was the same scolding, condescending tone Alonzo used with her when he wanted to make her feel small and stupid. "I didn't know," she said stiffly. "I've never had to know about rotting porch posts and cloudy windows before." All at once her throat went tight and she was afraid she'd cry.

"You certainly know about color," he said, surprising her again. "This room is very nice. I wouldn't have thought of gray, but the color works well in here."

The compliment made her throat relax and her taut nerves unwind. "Thank you."

"I'll go out and check out that window casing. Let me work up some numbers. I'll get back to you by the middle of next week."

"I'll be anxious to hear what you come up with."

As the door closed behind him, Frankie's thought swirled in her head, clamoring for her attention. One thing was for certain. She'd do whatever it took to save the porch. Wide and gracious, it was one of the reasons she'd bought the house in the first place. She regarded the stained carpeting. Knowing there was a hardwood floor hiding underneath it was definitely a game changer. She'd refinish it herself. That was going to save her a bundle. She hugged herself again. Her house. Her very own.

She was fifty years old and she'd never had a house of her own. The one in Cincinnati she'd shared with Alonzo for twenty years was his before they were married. He hadn't liked change, and had resisted all of her suggestions for remodeling. Before Alonzo, she'd always rented. But this house … this charming, crooked, wonderful, run-down house was hers.

And she'd bring it back to life, one project at a time.

She thought of Tracy Johanson, and how she'd noticed the way his big hands had caressed the hand hewn rafters. A small shadow of disappointment moved across her heart and she sighed. She'd also noticed he was wearing a wedding ring.

Chapter Two

According to their website, Saint Bridgette's Roman Catholic Church was located in the third block of Columbus Avenue, between the First Presbyterian and the Second Baptist Churches. Frankie had meant to drive by the day before to make sure she could find it, but between painting the living room and her appointment with Tracy Johanson, she hadn't gotten around to it.

Tracy Johanson.

Was it improper for her to be attracted to him, aside from the fact that he was married? A book she'd read said the acceptable time to start a new relationship after grieving the loss of a spouse was three hundred and sixty-five days. Alonzo had been gone for two hundred and twelve. She didn't really want a relationship, though. Just someone to have dinner with once in a while, maybe see a movie with here and there. Someone to ease the loneliness a little bit. And technically, she wasn't grieving.

She shook her head, disgusted with herself. Life had thrust her into the role of grieving widow, and she couldn't even do that right.

As soon as she turned onto Columbus Avenue, she saw the church steeples. In the third block, a sign in front of a towering, gray-stone church confirmed she was in the right place, so she pulled into the parking lot out back. She was fifteen minutes early, early enough for a few quiet moments of prayer before mass started. She went inside, admiring the gleaming stained glass windows and the planter boxes filled with pink and white flowers as she passed.

The church was absolutely gorgeous. So much grander than St. Sebastian's. She hoped the people would be friendly.

She picked up a bulletin from a table in the foyer and slid into a pew in the back of the church. Though the building would have held twice the number of parishioners as St. Sebastian's, there were only a couple dozen people in the pews, most of them elderly. She found that disappointing and felt a stab of homesickness. Though small, St. Sebastian's had been a thriving parish, full most every Sunday with young and old people alike.

Give this a chance, Frankie, she thought.

The service began with a lovely old pipe organ belting out her favorite hymn. A good sign, she thought. The priest, Father Joseph Quigley, looked about eighty years old, but surprisingly, his homily was up-to-date and engaging. He talked about waiting for God's timing, and not running ahead of Him. About how God always gives the best to those who trust him enough to wait for his leading. Frankie thought about that for a moment. Was that what she'd done, run ahead of God? If she'd waited, would a better man than Alonzo have come along? Would she have had the kind of marriage she always dreamed of?

She'd married Alonzo Bonetti when she was thirty because she felt like she was running out of time. He was ten years older than she was, successful and charming, and he promised her the moon. They had agreed to start a family right away, had even decided on names for their children. It wasn't until after their honeymoon that Alonzo confessed to having had a procedure years before. There wouldn't be any children. Ever. It was a crushing disappointment, the first of many lies he would tell her over the next twenty years.

When the service ended, Frankie left the church without anyone so much as glancing at her. She'd planned to go home and start tearing out the living room carpet, but the planter boxes at the church made her want to buy flowers for her yard instead. After a couple of wrong turns, she found the Home Depot and pulled into the parking lot.

The garden center was overwhelming. Flowers would cheer her up and add curb appeal to the house, but what should she buy?

She gravitated to a display of red, orange and gold colored azaleas. A glance at their tags told her they liked the sun, so she put one of each color in her cart. They would look pretty along the side of the house, where it was sunny for most of the afternoon.

She picked out a mixed flat of pansies to plant with them, loving that they looked like little dancing girls in colorful skirts. The front of the house was shaded almost entirely by a beautiful, gnarly old apple tree, so the attendant recommended hostas and impatiens. She selected a pretty variety of variegated green and white hostas, and filled a flat with a mix of red, pink and white impatiens. Stowing the plants in the trunk of her car, she bit her lip.

She'd forgotten about the porch. She'd have to hold off on planting the shade-loving things. They'd likely get trampled when Tracy came to do the work. She sighed. That was going to be an ever loving mess. And probably an expensive mess.

Even so, she was looking forward to having Tracy Johanson around. The realization pricked her conscience. He was married and that meant he was off limits.

I'm sorry, Lord. Please forgive me. Please help me to not be attracted to him.

•

On Sunday morning Tracy was at his kitchen table, paperwork spread out in front of him. He had a pencil in one hand and a cup of strong, black coffee in the other when his cell phone rang. A glance at the screen told him it was Rhoda calling. He put the phone on speaker and answered the call.

"What's up, little sister?"

"I'm calling to invite you for lunch. I have white chili in the crock pot, which you love. Plus you need a haircut, so I won't take no for an answer."

"I can't, Rho. I've got a job to finish up today."

"On Sunday?"

"I've got a deadline."

"Dinner, then?"

"We'll see."

"Deadline or not, you have to eat."

"I'll eat when I get this job in the books. I have to get it off my plate, since it looks like now I might have some extra jobs to fit into my already ridiculously full schedule."

"So you met with Francesca?"

"Yep."

"What did you think?"

"I think that house you sold her needs a lot of work."

"Well I know that. What did you think of Francesca? Isn't she great?"

All at once he got the sinking feeling he knew what the phone call was really about. "She seems fine."

"Fine?"

"Rhodie, don't."

"It's been four years, Trace. You need to take off that wedding ring and get back out there."

His jaw clenched. The straightforwardness that made Rhoda a top-notch realtor often made her a big pain in the butt as a sibling. "I'm not having this conversation with you."

"Okay, okay. But I think you should ask her out before someone else does."

"I'm ending this call now."

"Fine. Dinner is at six. I'll see you then," she said, ending the call.

"Way to get the last word in, Rhoda," he murmured.

Setting down the phone, he rubbed his eyes, all at once feeling tired. Rhoda was forty-four, six years younger than him, but for some reason she'd taken to mothering him after Joanne died. He knew she meant well, but her constant attempts at matchmaking got on his nerves. He knew it had been four years. He knew that. Since when was there a time limit on grief? As far as Tracy was concerned, forty years wouldn't be enough.

Setting thoughts of his sister aside, he went back to work on his figures. He'd crunched the numbers a half dozen times, trying to find ways to shave off some of the cost. The biggest expense would be the porch. He could do the other jobs alone, but for the porch he'd need another guy. And Lord knew what kind of rot might be lurking under that porch roof. He had four aluminum posts left over from another job. If Frankie liked them, that would save a couple hundred bucks. But by the time he bought the lumber and paid his help he'd almost have to eat his own labor to make it affordable.

Putting his pencil down, he took a swallow of coffee. He thought of Frankie, with her eager smile and her messy hair and those sad, beautiful eyes.

She was a beautiful woman, there was no denying that. A little flighty, maybe, but she had something, some endearing quality he couldn't quite name. If he was going to date again, which he wasn't – he was too old and too tired to put forth the effort—but if he ever got to the point of wanting to date again, he would date someone like Frankie Bonetti.

•

When Frankie got home from the store it was after two o'clock. Probably too hot for planting, she thought, but she could at least dig the holes. She went inside, took off her church clothes, and changed into a pair of old jeans and a tee shirt. She returned to the car, unloaded the flowers, trowels, and other garden tools she'd bought, and carried them to the yard. This was going to be fun!

Fifteen minutes into the project she found it wasn't as easy as she'd imagined. The ground along the side of the house was hard and clay-packed. She'd bought the soil booster the attendant at the Home Depot had recommended but digging up the soil in order to mix it in was killing her. As she stabbed the end of her trowel into the ground, she felt a spasm in her lower back. Wincing, she massaged the tender spot. Her body's painful little reminders always took her by surprise. They made her remember she was not young anymore. Not old, at fifty. But not the energetic, supple woman she'd been, even at forty.

Hearing sirens, she glanced up to see two patrol cars shrieking down the street. Sirens had always made her uneasy. They made her think of things like drug raids, robberies, and domestic violence. Saying a little prayer for whoever was in trouble, she went back to her digging.

On the corner of Cleveland Avenue and Cottage Street, Frankie's house was in a middle zone; a pocket two blocks wide that sat between Port Arthur's two very different worlds. Five blocks north, Where Cleveland Avenue met Candlewick Street, the houses became strikingly beautiful. Five blocks south, at Hunter, they became sad and shabby. Holy Child Academy, the school where she would be working in the fall, was a block south of Hunter Street, on Toledo Avenue. She hoped she would be safe there.

By the time she got the soil prepared the sky had clouded over and the weather was much cooler, so she decided to plant the flowers after all. When she'd lovingly set them in their holes and given them a good soaking, she stood back to admire the effect. It was charming, as she'd known it would be.

She backed up to the sidewalk to get the full picture. The reds, golds and oranges of the azaleas were a nice pop of color against the house's cream siding, and the pansies added interesting splashes of purple and white. The flowers had taken the space from blah to beautiful. Maybe she would add a bird bath and try to attract a few birds. It would be lovely to watch them from the window.

A woman walked toward her, carrying a canvas grocery bag, and Frankie smiled at her.

"Hello."

The woman stopped and nodded at the flowers. "That looks real nice, honey."

Frankie beamed. "Thank you! I really don't know very much about flowers at all. I just liked the colors. I dream of a gorgeous, colorful yard, but I have no idea how to get there."

"You know them are spring flowers, don't you? The azaleas will stay green, but the colors won't last. If you put in some zinnias and cone flowers later, you can keep your color going right on up 'till fall."

"I didn't know that."

The woman cocked her head and studied the space. "Maybe you could get you a bird feeder or a bird bath. Make it a cute little garden spot."

"I was just thinking the same thing!" Delighted, she took a

good look at the woman. She was older than Frankie, maybe sixty or sixty-five. Her face was lined, and steely gray curls peeked out from beneath the scarf she wore on her head. Her dress looked like a Lula Roe, but one that came from a thrift store. It was faded, the hem frayed where it hit the tops of her blue crocks. But she had amazing eyes. Doe eyes, Frankie thought, kind and gentle and wise. "You must know a lot about flowers."

"My daddy owned a nursery, years ago. Me and my sisters grew up with dirt underneath our fingernails and seeds in our hair. He named us all after flowers. I'm Lilly."

"It sounds like a nice way to grow up, Lilly. I'm Frankie Bonetti. The son my father never had." She stuck out her hand and shook Lilly's warm, thin one.

Before she knew it, she and Lilly had moved into the back yard. Most of the sunlight out back was blotted out by a narrow, two-story barn. Rhoda had told her that when the house was built, a hundred years before, the barn had been home to a horse and buggy.

Over the years, the structure had served as a candle shop, an art studio, and an antiques shop, but it hadn't been anything but empty for over a decade. The listing had marketed it as income potential, but even Frankie could see that the old barn would need a lot of work before it resembled anything usable.

She suspected most potential buyers had seen it as an eyesore, an expensive nuisance to be removed. Even Rhoda had suggested tearing it down and putting up a small garage instead. But Frankie thought the old barn was fabulous. She dreamed of one day starting her own catering business. Restored and reconfigured, the barn would be the perfect place. She was given to flights of fancy lately. All of her old dreams had grown wings, now that Alonzo was not there to squash them.

"Me, I'd put in a cottage garden, right off that deck," Lilly said. She suggested herbs and mints, bachelor buttons and coreopsis and other flowers Frankie wasn't familiar with. "You could get you a little fountain with running water and put it in the middle. And a lilac tree. And as long as we're dreaming, I think a nice pergola with a swing would fit out yonder behind the barn. I do love me a swing."

"It all sounds wonderful," Frankie said. "But I have so much work to do inside the house, it'll probably be ten years before I can even think about a pergola."

Lilly's doe eyes regarded her for a long moment, then she smiled and picked up the shopping bag from where she'd set it on the ground. Frankie noticed it held a loaf of bread and six cans of tuna. "Must be you got a good job, to do all that remodeling."

"Actually, I don't know if it's a good job or not. I haven't started it yet. I've only lived here for a couple of weeks."

"I didn't think you seemed like you was from around here."

"I've lived in Cincinnati my whole life, up until now."

Lilly hooted. "Girl, what are you doing in Port Arthur?"

She hesitated. The old Frankie would have blurted out the whole story from start to finish. But she was going to be better about that. She was going to develop a filter. "My husband passed away in October. After that, the house was too big, too much for me. The city was too big." She shrugged. "I needed a change."

"Lordy, I'd say you got you one."

"I'll be starting at Holy Child Academy at the end of August. It's over on Toledo Avenue."

"I know where it is. You a teacher, then?"

"No. Actually I'll be…" She stopped herself before saying she'd be overseeing the culinary arts department. That's what Alonzo always told people when they asked about her work at St. Sebastian's. As if food service was an embarrassment. As if saying culinary arts made the job more important. To Frankie, it was important.

The kids loved her homemade lasagna and Johnny Marzetti, and she loved providing them with delicious, healthy meals every day. She was making a new life now, done trying to live up to Alonzo's impossible standards. "I'm going to be working in the cafeteria."

"You get free food?"

The question surprised her. "I imagine I'll get free lunches. I mean, I always did at my old school."

"That's good, then. Sounds like you got you a good job."

Lilly hitched the bag onto her shoulder. "It's been nice talking to you, but I better get on home now. If you need someone to mow your lawn this summer, I know a couple of guys."

"I'll surely keep that in mind. I hope you'll stop by again, Lilly. Stop by any time. I could use some more landscaping advice."

Lilly smiled. "I'll do that, Frankie Bonetti."

Frankie watched as Lilly trudged off down the sidewalk. She hugged herself again. She'd made her first friend in Port Arthur.

Chapter Three

The house had been on the market for one hundred days when Frankie first noticed it. She'd been leaving Port Arthur after interviewing for a position at Holy Child when the little house on Cottage Street beckoned to her. It was a crisp January day and a dusting of snow on the apple tree and the red tin roof made the house seem snug and cozy.

That evening she'd searched for the listing online. That the house went up for sale the very day Alonzo died had seemed significant to her. From the photos, the house looked cozy inside, too, if a bit rundown. The property was priced to sell, and it needed her and rundown or not, Frankie was determined to give it a second chance. She didn't know, that day, that the porch roof was caving in, or how miserably difficult removing the living room carpeting would be.

Monday morning, armed with a carpet knife and a brand new box of blades, she plunged into the job. She'd been given a list of guidelines when she set up her account with the city utility department. Old carpeting had to be cut into three-foot squares, rolled, and tied with string in order to be accepted for pickup.

Even with the new blades, cutting through the carpet was murder. But each new square she removed exposed another block of wooden planks. It was like opening a Christmas present each time, and the pure satisfaction of it kept her going. The planks were scuffed and splattered with paint, but so far there didn't seem to be any that were damaged.

Two hours into the project her back was screaming and her hands were blistered, but she persevered. In her mind, she imagined gleaming mahogany planks, as smooth as glass, and how she would show the floor off to Tracy Johanson and tell him, Oh, it really wasn't that much work at all. He would admire the floor. He would complement her again.

A twinge of guilt intruded on her lovely daydream. This was not right, any way you looked at it. She was not only running ahead of God this time, she was barreling face first into the tenth commandment. Thou shall not covet they neighbor's ... husband.

"I'm sorry, Lord," she whispered, and quickly adjusted the fantasy to one where she showed off the floor to Rhoda instead.

Another hour and she was finished. With the last of the carpet removed, she rolled up the pieces, tied them with twine, and lugged them out to the curb.

Back inside, she could see how beautiful the floor was going to be. There were spots in which the old varnish clung to the wood, and the entire floor was busy with white footprints, as if someone had spilled paint and tracked it all through the room. It was going to take a whole lot more work to get it to look like the vision in her head, but she would do it! She'd go out and rent a sander and get after those footprints. But first, coffee. And a shower. It was sweaty, dirty work and she felt like a hot mess.

She'd just measured out the coffee and poured in the water when she heard a sharp rapping at her front door. She hurried back to the living room. Maybe the new curtains she'd ordered for the living room had arrived. She peeked out the window and her heart sank straight to her toes. A white pickup truck sat in front of the house, the words Johanson General Contracting written on the side.

Oh, no!

Her first impulse was to run and hide. She couldn't let Tracy see her like this. But everyone knew how contractors were. They were busy men. If she didn't answer the door he would simply go on to the next job and Lord knew when he'd get back to her. She desperately wanted to know what kind of price he'd come up with, had been in knots imagining what the improvements would cost, so she swallowed her pride and opened the door.

He looked amazing. His face was clean shaven and his hair, cut short. She noticed his glance move over her and cringed. Hot mess, she thought.

"Good morning. I worked up those figures for you. Is now a good time to go over them?"

She scraped her hair back behind her ears. "Sure. Come in."

He took a step inside. "You got the carpet torn out. This is going to be nice."

"You think so?"

"No marks or gouges. Looks like they set the carpet right on top of the floor without putting down plywood, so you don't have any nail holes to fill." He dropped to a squat and scraped at the paint with his thumb nail. "At least it's latex. It should scrub right off."

There was an awkward silence. She thought of telling him about cutting the squares and how each new area of unspoiled hardwood she uncovered had seemed like a gift. But she'd made up her mind she wasn't going to babble any more. "Why don't we go over your figures at the kitchen table? I was just going to have a cup of coffee. Would you like one?"

"Sure."

She opened the cupboard and took down the only two mugs she'd unpacked so far. The Mickey and Minnie Mouse mugs she'd gotten years ago on a trip to Walt Disney World. She poured them full of coffee and handed him one, hoping he wouldn't see that her hands were shaking.

"Mickey Mouse, huh?"

The cup looked like a child's plaything in his big hands. As they closed around Mickey's stupidly grinning face, she fought a fit of nervous giggles. "They were on the top of the box. I haven't unpacked most of my things yet."

He opened the ledger he'd brought, at once all business. "Okay, here's what I've come up with. These are worst case and best case scenarios, depending on what I run into."

She scanned the list detailing the costs of labor and materials for each job. The window. The laundry room ceiling. The bath tub and the stair railing. "These look about like what I expected," she said, relieved.

"If we do the porch, I'll get new jacks. We can use them in the basement later to replace the ones that are rusting. The cost of those is minimal." He pulled a second sheet of paper from the ledger and set it on the table in front of her.

She scanned the estimate, written in bold, black ink. Bracing herself, she glanced at the total cost at the bottom of the page. Her breath escaped in a rush. It was more than she wanted to spend right now, but so much less than she'd even dared hope it might be.

"It looks do-able," she said. "In fact it looks very do-able."

He smiled. "I have four aluminum posts left over from a job I did a couple of years ago. They're an odd height, so I haven't been able to use them, but I think they'd work for this house just fine. They're taking up space in my warehouse, so I'd practically give them to you. But if you don't like the style of them, we can buy different ones. Of course, that will add to the cost." He opened his ledger and pulled out a picture. "They're similar to these."

They weren't anything she would have picked out, but they weren't bad. They were a chunky, modern style column, much more modern that the existing wooden newel posts. These were different, but that didn't make them wrong. "I like them," she said.

He rewarded her with another smile. "Good, then."

"When can you start the work?"

"I'll pick up the lumber later today and leave it on your front porch, if that's okay."

"Of course."

"My schedule's pretty jammed up right now, to be honest. But we could start as early as tomorrow, if you don't mind us working evenings, say around five-thirty?"

"I don't mind at all."

"We like to make use of every minute of daylight and dry weather this time of year."

"I can imagine. Thanks so much for getting back to me so quickly."

When he left, she chanced a glance in the mirror. She saw with dismay that her hair was limp and stringy and her face, streaked with dirt. A hot, filthy mess. "That's what you get," she told the woman in the mirror. "That's just what you get for running ahead of God."

●

She was a beauty. And it wasn't just the haphazard loveliness on the outside. Frankie Bonetti had a beautiful heart. She exuded an inner warmth, a transparency you didn't often find. There wasn't an ounce of pretense to her. What you saw was what you got.

Tracy turned down Youngstown Boulevard, where his crew was hanging drywall in the mayor's new addition. It was an important job and he wanted to make sure it was done right.

His brow furrowed. He'd be lucky to break even on the porch, but he was way overdue in the good deeds department. And the look on her face—relief, an almost childlike joy— knowing he'd been the one to put it there would be payment enough.

He pulled into the mayor's driveway and took out his cell phone. Pal answered on the first ring. "I'm glad you're still there," Tracy said. "There's an order on my desk. I need you to pick that up at Cunningham's and drop it off at 388 Cleveland Avenue. Just leave it on the porch."

"Will do, boss."

He ended the call. Immediately his phone rang. Rhoda. Ignoring it, he stuffed the phone in his pocket. She'd started in again about Frankie after dinner last night. He'd shut the conversation down, but he knew his sister was right. Frankie was a nice looking woman. If he didn't ask her out, someone else surely would.

Maybe he should take a chance. Just dinner. No nonsense. No jumping through hoops. It would be nice to have a woman's companionship again. And he knew in his heart that Rhoda was right about another thing. It had been four long years. It was time for him to move on.

●

Frankie stood beneath the hot spray of the shower, feeling

satisfaction as the morning's sweat and grime washed away down the drain. He said he would be dropping off the materials later that day. This time she would be ready.

She stepped from the shower, dried off, and wrapped her hair in a towel. She retrieved her makeup bag from the drawer and brushed a coat of mascara on her lashes.

The woman in the mirror stared at her, disapproval in her eyes. "It's just mascara," she told the woman. "I'm not going to pursue him. I would never do that. I just want to look presentable, for once."

Dressed in a clean pair of leggings and her favorite top, she fluffed her hair and tried to decide how to make use of the time. She wouldn't do anything that would cause her to get dirty, that was for sure. Wandering through the house, she opened the guest room door. It was full of boxes, things she hadn't had the emotional stamina to unpack and go through yet.

"No time like the present," she murmured.

Grabbing a box labeled *kitchen*, she carried it to the table. Opening the flaps, she saw that it contained her coffee mugs. Smiling, she ran a sink full of water and began to wash them.

After she had unpacked, washed, and put away three boxes of kitchen items, she started on her clothes. She'd gained ten pounds since Alonzo's funeral, no longer seeing any reason to deny herself the cakes and cannoli's she adored.

She didn't mind a little extra weight. Alonzo had always wanted her to be a size smaller than she could comfortably maintain. But she was sorry to have to get rid of the clothes, some of which she'd barely worn. She picked out a few things she thought she might be able to sell on e-bay and stuffed the rest in a bag for Goodwill. She'd just bagged the last item when she heard a truck pull up out front.

Her heart fluttering like a mad butterfly, she blew out a breath, smoothed back her hair, and went outside. A man was busily loading things onto her porch: two by fours, floor jacks, and Lord knew what else, but she saw with disappointment that it wasn't Tracy.

"Hello," she said uncertainly.

The man turned. He was taller than Tracy, lean and lanky,

with brown eyes and caramel colored hair that was easily three months overdue for a cut.

"Well hello there!" The glance that swept over her was so appreciative it embarrassed her.

"You're not Tracy."

He laughed. "Not hardly. I'm Pal Wainright, Tracy's right hand man. I'll be working on this project with him."

"It's nice to meet you."

When he'd finished unloading the truck, he lingered. "So we're rebuilding your porch, huh?"

"Yep."

He studied the rotting beams, then his gaze returned to her face. "Not a minute too soon, from the looks. You shouldn't have ever let it get this bad."

She forced a smile. "I've only owned the house for a couple of weeks. If you'll excuse me, I was just on my way out."

"Sure thing. I guess I'll see you tomorrow, Mrs.?"

"Bonetti."

"All righty, Mrs. Bonetti. You stay off this porch until then, okay?" He winked at her, embarrassing her further.

"I'll do that. Goodbye, Pal."

She grabbed her car keys from the table inside the door, closed it, and walked away. She drove around for fifteen minutes, until she was sure he would be gone, before going back home. He didn't seem a bad sort, just not the kind of man she wanted to pass the time of day with. When she returned home his truck was gone, so she pulled in the driveway, scolding herself for her silliness. She was certainly under no obligation to chat with a man she didn't even know. She would need to be more assertive from now on. Noticing that her azalea plants looked droopy, she filled a watering can and carried it to the side of the house. Lilly was coming down the sidewalk, pulling what looked to be a child's red wagon.

"Hello, Lilly!"

"Hello yourself, Frankie Bonetti!" She parked the wagon under the apple tree and walked to where Frankie stood. "Just so you know, it's better to wait for evening to water. It's mighty hot out here, especially for May."

Lilly wore the same dress as the day before. Her face was

shiny with sweat and Frankie noticed that her ankles looked swollen. Whatever she had in that wagon must have been heavy. "It sure is. Can I offer you a glass of lemonade?"

"That'd be real nice."

"I'll get us each a glass. We can't sit on my porch, as you can see, there's no room. But I'll bring a couple of chairs out and we can sit under the apple tree. There's a nice breeze out front this time of day."

When she and Lilly were seated with their drinks, she started telling Lilly about the project, and about the strange man who'd delivered her materials.

"Wainright, huh? You sure he ain't Mister Right?"

"Oh, Lilly, no! No way!"

They laughed a good, old-fashioned belly laugh.

"Speaking of Mister Right, I was actually hoping to see you today. I got a couple of boys I want you to meet."

She watched as Lilly walked to the wagon and retrieved the large box. She carried it back to where Frankie sat and placed it in her lap. It wasn't a bit heavy, and Frankie cautiously pulled back the flaps. Two small kittens squinted up at her.

"Oh," she cried. "Who are you?" She lifted out a gray and black tabby and cuddled it close to her chest with one hand, softly stroking the little orange kitten in the box with the other.

"Like I said, just a couple little fellows I thought might be nice company for ya."

"Where did you get them?"

"Their mama got hit in the road out in front of my place. Her and two other kittens."

"Oh, you poor sweet babies," Frankie crooned.

"I been feeding them, but I really can't have 'em where I am. Do you like either one of them?"

Frankie had always adored cats. She'd had a calico as a little girl. The cat lived for twelve years, and when it developed diabetes and she'd had to have it put to sleep, she'd cried for a month. After leaving home, she'd lived in a series of apartments, none of which allowed pets, and when she'd moved into Alonzo's house and asked about getting a kitten he wouldn't hear of it. He gave her a detailed list of why it wasn't a good idea —they'd have to deal with a litter box, cats did hundreds of dollars' worth of damage to furniture and draperies with their claws, the vet visits would put them in the poor house, and on and on. She knew it was out of the question and she hadn't asked again. But this was her house. And her house needed a cat. Maybe even two.

"I like them both," she said. "Actually, I love them."

"You'd be doing me a favor to take 'em."

"Let me pay you for them, Lilly. They'd be twenty or thirty dollars each if I got them from the rescue."

Lilly stiffened and her voice took on a surprising sharpness. "I don't need your money, Frankie. I didn't come here to sell them to you. I wanted to give them to you, as a gift."

"Okay. Well, thank you."

"You're welcome."

As quickly as that, the sharp edge smoothed away and she was Lilly again. They chatted for a moment more, until the kittens started mewling relentlessly. "I should probably take these boys inside and get them a drink of water."

"Probably ought to." Lilly stood. "I should be getting home anyway."

A thought occurred to Frankie. "Lilly, are you going to be passing the Goodwill on your way home?"

"Yes."

"I've been unpacking and I have a bag of things that don't fit me anymore. Would you drop them off for me?"

"Sure thing."

She took the kittens inside, then went to the guest room and retrieved the small bag of clothes she'd set aside for e-bay. She dared not risk offending Lilly again by offering her free clothes. But if she happened to look in the bag and see something she liked… She took the bag outside and set it in the wagon. "Thanks, Lilly. And thanks again for the kittens."

"What're you gonna name them?"

She smiled. "Pepper and Nutmeg."

Lilly chuckled. "You're a good one, Frankie Bonetti!" She pulled the wagon onto the sidewalk and trudged away, and Frankie hurried inside, anxious to see if the kittens would like their new names.

Chapter Four

It stormed all night and all the next morning. Frankie listened to the sound of the rain drumming on her roof and hoped it didn't mean the work on the porch would be delayed.

After coffee and a shower, she slogged to the grocery store for a litter box, kitten food, and some cat toys. It seemed like a good day to make bread so she added flour and yeast to her cart as well. As an afterthought, she bought a package of chicken, a bag of potato chips, and a jar of dill pickle spears. The men would get hungry while they worked. Maybe they would want sandwiches later.

Back home she filled the box with litter and showed it to the cats. To her amazement they used it on the first try.

"What smart little boys you are," she said. She kissed them both, then presented each with a rubber mouse, and went to the kitchen to start her bread.

When the dough was ready she covered it and set it on the stove to rise, then returned to the guest room. Yesterday's progress had encouraged her and she wanted to keep going. And besides, her back was still sore from cutting up the carpet. The thought of scrubbing away a hundred footprints today was more than she could bear.

She sorted box after box, putting things into piles. She'd read an article about decluttering. It said if an item no longer brought you joy you were supposed to thank it for its service and send it on its way. She discovered she really didn't want many of the things that had been in Alonzo's house. This was her house and they just didn't fit here. She felt silly, but she dutifully thanked each item as she set it aside; the crystal candlesticks, the heavy, floral oil paintings, the silver bud vases. When she'd boxed them back up and marked them for donation she felt remarkably cleansed. She wouldn't even take the time to try and sell them. She'd just give them away.

At four-thirty, with the guest room well on its way to purged and two loaves of bread cooling on racks, she loaded the boxes in her car and headed for Goodwill. The article also said that once you purged you should get rid of the unwanted items right away, before you changed your mind.

It had stopped raining while she worked. The sun peeked through the hazy sky, creating a rainbow. Frankie took this to be a good sign, somehow.

At five forty-five Tracy knocked on her door.

"We're going to go ahead and get started," he told her. "You're gonna hear some noise out here, but don't be alarmed."

"I'll try not to be," Frankie told him, already alarmed by the faint scent of his cologne and the way his black tee shirt hugged the contours of his big arms.

She watched from the window as the two men put the first jack in place. With a shove, the old post fell away with a crash, crumbling to dust when it hit the ground. After that she couldn't watch any more. She turned the radio on, and then switched it off again. She could hear Tracy and Pal talking through her open window and she liked the steady rhythm of their conversation. Taking out the chicken she'd boiled earlier, she cut it into chunks and added mayonnaise, onions and celery.

By seven-thirty the talking seemed to have stopped. She ventured outside to find the two men sitting on the porch, drinking bottles of water. The old posts lay in pieces on the ground. In their place stood four shiny, red jacks.

"Wow."

"It's a good thing they sold this house when they did," Tracy said. "Or they'd have been selling it without a porch. Those posts were rotted through. It was only a matter of time until they collapsed, taking the roof with them."

"This looks like a lot of work," Frankie said.

"Nah."

Pal was staring at her like he'd never seen a woman before.

Embarrassed, she turned back to Tracy. "You haven't eaten yet, have you? I made chicken salad, if you're hungry."

"I'm hungry," Pal piped up.

She returned to the kitchen and cut the bread into thick slices, added the chicken salad, and put the sandwiches on a tray with the chips and pickle spears she'd bought.

"This was sure nice of you, Frankie," Pal said. "I don't remember nobody ever feeding us before, do you, Trace?"

"No, I don't."

She'd made them two sandwiches each and she noted with satisfaction that when they were done, not a single crumb was left on the tray.

"That was delicious," Pal said. "Your husband is a lucky man."

"I'm a widow."

"Oh. Sorry to hear that."

Frankie didn't think he looked a bit sorry.

Tracy stood. "Thank you, Frankie. That hit the spot. Pal, what do you say we call it a day?"

"Ready whenever you are, boss." But he didn't seem ready. He stood on the porch, staring at Frankie and shifting in his work boots. "Uh, Frankie?"

She looked at him, eyebrows raised.

"Hey, it was nice of you to give us sandwiches and all. Maybe I'll pay you back by taking you out for dinner. How's Saturday night sound?"

In the silence that followed, she glanced at Tracy. He looked as thunderstruck as she felt.

"Oh, umm…"

It had been a long time since she'd been asked out on a date. So long that she couldn't remember the last time. She didn't care much for Pal Wainright, but he looked so hopeful just then that she couldn't bear to turn him down. What would one date hurt?

"Sure, why not?"

His face broke into a wide grin. "Cool. Where do you want to go?"

"I'm not sure what my choices are."

"Why don't the two of you figure that out later?" Tracy

said curtly. Without another word he turned and strode to his truck. Frankie watched him climb in. Was he angry? Did he not like his workers dating clients?

"You think about it and let me know." Pal made a gun with his thumb and index finger and shot her. "Don't you go changing your mind, now."

Lord have mercy. She got the feeling Saturday was going to be a long night.

When she went back inside she discovered the kittens had found her bowl of potpourri and strewn it all over the living room.

She scooped Nutmeg up and scolded him. "It's a good thing God made you cute, because you're as naughty as sin." She stroked his fur while Pepper rubbed around her ankles. "I should probably just stick to cats. You're affectionate and playful and you never make me feel nervous." She set the wiggling kitten down, thinking about her date and wondering what she'd gotten herself into.

After a good night's sleep she didn't feel any better about her upcoming date with Pal Wainright. The book she'd read said to start with small, nonthreatening scenarios, such as a walk around the neighborhood, or a cup of coffee in a crowded café, and only to date men you genuinely wanted to spend time with. Right out of the gate she'd done it wrong. Oh well. Maybe Pal would grow on her.

Sitting down at her computer, she watched a Youtube tutorial that recommended using a sanding block when removing old varnish from a hardwood floor. Maybe she'd do that, rather than rent a sander. But first she'd have to see about those footprints.

The latex came off easily with an S.O.S. pad and some elbow grease, and to her delight, the old varnish lifted off with it. Before she knew it, every last trace of paint was gone. Next she'd have to select a stain color. But not today. Her hard work over the past few days was catching up with her and she was beyond tired. The kittens were stalking the bowl of potpourri, so she shut them in the guest room and went outside to sit on her porch.

It was a beautiful spring afternoon and the neighborhood

was busy with activity. There were people walking dogs, kids riding bicycles and skateboards, neighbors hanging over fences to chat with one another. From a short distance she saw Lilly coming down the sidewalk, her red wagon rattling along behind her. As she drew closer, Frankie saw that it was full of empty pop cans.

"Those are some nice looking porch posts you got there, Frankie Bonetti!" she called.

"They're temporary, but at least they're stable. Can you sit for a minute?"

As Lilly stepped up onto the porch, Frankie noticed she was wearing one of the tops from the bag she'd given her.

Lilly mopped her face with a hankie. "This breeze is heaven. How's my boys?"

"They're wonderfully naughty."

She sank down in a chair. "Hey, why'd you give them clothes away? They're just like new. You rich folks..." She shook her head.

"I'm hardly rich, Lilly. I told you the clothes didn't fit me anymore. I've gained some weight since my husband died."

"You mind if I took some things for myself?"

"Of course not. Let me get us some lemonade."

She poured two tall glasses and put them on a tray with a plate of biscotti. "You can help me eat these, too," she said, setting the tray on a table beside Lilly. "Before I gain another ten pounds."

Lilly accepted the drink and two pieces of biscotti.

"What are you up to today?" Frankie asked.

"Just picking up some cans to scrap. I might go to the library, too."

"Do you like to read?"

"Not so much. But it's cool in there, and they've got good magazines."

Silence fell, but it was a comfortable silence. Frankie felt no need to babble with Lilly.

"How long did you say your husband's been gone?" Lilly asked.

"Since October."

"Ooh, that's not long."

"No."

"My Harvey has been gone for sixteen years."

Frankie took a sip of lemonade. She didn't want to be like Pal and offer an automatic, insincere condolence. She tried to imagine what it would be like to lose a beloved husband. She imagined it would be torture. "I'm so sorry," she finally said.

"Don't be. Harvey was an ornery, good-for-nothing bum."

Unable to hold it back, Frankie sprayed out the lemonade she'd been drinking. Giggles she could not control bubbled up inside her and burst from her lips.

"Now why don't you tell me how you really feel?"

Lilly chuckled. Then she laughed, feeding Frankie's laughter until neither of them could catch their breath. Oh, it felt good to laugh. It had been so long. All of the anxiety and fear and stress of the past few months seemed to come pouring out of her in the release of that beautiful, spontaneous laughter. When she'd composed herself, Frankie dabbed at her eyes with a napkin and pulled in a shuddering breath.

"My Alonzo… He died in bed with a prostitute."

"Oh now—" Suddenly Lilly roared, and it started Frankie up again. It wasn't funny. It wasn't a bit funny, but somehow all of the pain and humiliation was soothed. Lilly's laughter made it seem smaller somehow, less horrible.

Finally spent, Frankie rested her head against the back of her chair. "I'm in a mess, Lil."

"What's wrong, honey?"

"I've got a date Saturday night."

"Dang, girl. What's wrong with that?"

"It's with the wrong man."

"Not What's-his-name? Wayne Wrong?"

"I'm afraid so. I so don't want to go out with him."

"Then why did you say you would?"

"Because I'm a darn people-pleaser, that's why. I have been my whole life. What am I going to do?"

"Listen up, Frankie. You're going to go out with him. You're going to let him spend some money on you, show you a good time. You don't have to marry the man."

"Oh, but he's so goofy. You have no idea."

"They're all goofy, one way or another ain't they?"

She thought of calm, capable Tracy. *Not all of them.*

"I guess," she said.

"Where's he taking you?"

"I don't know. I'm supposed to decide but I don't know of any good places here."

"Ooh—tell him you want to go to Sloppy Sue's."

She cut Lilly a sideways glance. "Sloppy Sue's?"

"Honey, they got the best baby back ribs in the state of O-hio. Cornbread drowning in butter. Coleslaw tangy enough to make your toes tingle. M-m-m! I do love me some ribs. So you go eat you some good food, maybe listen to some music after that, and at the end of the night, it's 'get outta town, clown,' just like that old song says."

Frankie laughed. "I can't do that."

"Sure you can. Wainwrong'll get over it. Honey, you deserve this."

•

On Wednesday and Thursday Frankie kept herself busy putting away the things she'd decided to keep and cleaning the guest room, which was now empty of clutter. She played with the kittens and took long walks in the evenings, careful to be gone from five to seven thirty each night. By Friday evening at eight o'clock the porch was nearly finished. All four posts were in place.

Tracy had built a platform for the floor and boxed in a section of the ceiling to support them. She heard a knock at the door and opened it to see him standing there. "Do you want to come out and take a look at this?" he asked.

She stepped onto the porch. "Wow."

"Things went a lot more smoothly than I thought they would. There was no rot at the roofline, surprisingly, so we just had to build up the floor and the ceiling to even out the low spots where the house has settled. We should be able to wrap it up on Monday. You can pay the balance then."

"It looks beautiful. Just like a brand new porch!"

"Good. Don't worry about the gray on the posts, that's just primer. Do you want them white, like the old ones?" He was businesslike, not unfriendly, exactly, but not nearly as warm as he'd been a few days before. He was so good-looking it hurt.

"White will be fine."

"Okay. We'll get it calked and painted, fill in the nail holes, and you'll be in business."

"Wonderful."

"I'll see you next week then." He stepped from the porch and walked to his truck. Pal lingered.

"We still on for tomorrow night?"

"You bet." Her smile felt tight and unnatural but Pal didn't seem to notice.

"Good. Did you decide where you want to go?"

"Sloppy Sue's."

She saw absolute surprise on his face. "The rib place out on Ashtabula?"

"I don't know where it is."

He shrugged. "Okay, if that's what you want, then Sloppy Sue's it is. How about I pick you up at seven?"

"I'll be ready."

He made the gun with his fingers and shot her again, then walked to the truck, whistling. He climbed in, said something to Tracy, and they drove away. She stood, wistfully watching after them, her head filled with if onlys…

•

Pal was on cloud nine. Tracy, not so much.

He'd barely eaten since the sandwiches Frankie had made them a few nights before. His stomach was a mess and so were his nerves. This is why he hadn't wanted to think about a relationship. He didn't need the stress of it, or the drama. Or the disappointment. But it had worked out for the best. He could plainly see that now.

Dating was a young man's game and he didn't have the energy for it. It was a young man's game and he refused to act like an old fool.

But if he was going to date, he sure had enough sense not to take a woman like Frankie Bonetti to Sloppy Sue's. It was the biggest dive in Port Arthur. What was Pal thinking? Tracy was sure Pal was thrilled to be getting out of the date so cheaply, but even so…

Tracy wasn't made that way. If it was him going out for dinner with Frankie, he would do it right. He'd take her to a nice restaurant. The way he'd planned to before Pal cut in line ahead of him.

Chapter Five

If she'd been going out to dinner with Alonzo, Frankie's choice of clothing would have been simple. They'd have gone someplace like Primavera, and she'd have worn an ankle length skirt, a loose fitting blouse with a camisole, and a strand of pearls or a simple gold chain. She'd looked Sloppy Sue's up online, and it didn't look like a skirt and heels kind of place. It didn't look like any kind of place she'd ever eaten, and she hoped Lilly hadn't steered her wrong.

She finally settled on a pair of fitted jeans and a red cold shoulder top. When Pal arrived at seven o'clock, she was just finishing her make up. He wore faded jeans and a short sleeved polo shirt, so she felt good about her choices.

"You look great," he said.

"Thank you."

He thrust a bouquet of painted daisies at her. "I brought flowers."

"Thank you so much. They're lovely."

He waited in the living room while she went to find a vase. When she returned, he was studying her paint job. "Gray walls, huh?"

"They were beige when I moved in. The gray is so much more soothing. They say gray is the new white, whatever that means."

"Well, you just recently became a widow, so, I get it."

What was that supposed to mean? Before she could respond, he pointed at the floor. "What happened here?"

"Nothing, yet. I'm going to refinish the old hardwood."

"Or you could just put down carpet."

She felt her blood pressure kick up a notch. "I just tore out the carpet. I love hardwood floors."

He glanced around the room. "This place isn't half bad inside. With a little bit of work, you could flip it and buy something nicer. If it was me, I'd knock down that old barn in the yard and use the beams on these ceilings. Now that would look nice"

"I want to keep the barn. I might open a catering business some day."

He stared at her as if she'd grown a second head. "That's dumb. For what it would cost to restore that old barn you might better put up a steel building."

She counted to ten, trying hard not to let her anger win out over politeness. "Pal, can we go now?"

Out in Pal's truck, an uncomfortable silence enveloped them that even Frankie couldn't think how to fill. Thankfully it was a short drive to the restaurant.

"Here we are," Pal said, pulling into the rutted parking lot. Frankie's stared at the restaurant in disbelief. Sloppy Sue's was the eyesore of Ashtabula Avenue; a garish blue building, its sign depicting a pair of lips parted in a wide smile to reveal teeth stained with barbecue sauce. A tableful of men sat drinking beer on the porch out front, wearing wife beaters and cut-off jeans. They stopped talking when Frankie walked past, and their silence made her feel naked.

Inside, the restaurant was only slightly more appealing. Or maybe it was just too dark to see. A hostess handed them a pair of greasy menus and seated them at a table that looked out on the street. Glancing around, she couldn't help seeing Sloppy Sue's through Alonzo's eyes; the dirty, frayed carpeting and the torn upholstery on the stools that lined the bar. What had Lilly been thinking?

"Gonna go for the ribs?" Pal asked.

"Probably," Frankie took out her reading glasses and scanned her menu. "I've heard they're pretty good here."

"I dunno." He opened his menu. "Almost fifty years I've lived in this town, and I can't say I've ever been in here even once."

When the waitress returned they each ordered a beer and

a rack of ribs. She scooped up their menus, set a platter of cornbread on the table, and scurried away.

Needing something to do with her hands, Frankie cut through the lovely, brown crust of the bread and buttered them each a slice. She bit tentatively into hers, and the cornbread's sweet, cakelike texture flooded over her taste buds. Lilly was right about one thing, Sue's cornbread was out of this world.

"Not bad," Pal said. He polished off his slice and cut another. "So how long were you married?"

Frankie cleared her throat. "Twenty years."

"Same as me," he said.

She'd been afraid she would have to give him a sugar-coated version of her life with Alonzo, but Pal didn't ask a single question more about her marriage. She soon discovered that he had a two-track mind. His first track was his ex-wife, Candy. His second was Ohio State.

Frankie was proud of the Buckeyes. The whole state of Ohio was proud of the Buckeyes. But football was something she'd never been able to make any sense of.

The dinner conversation started with talk about the different players and coaches, their strengths and weaknesses. Pal went on to catalogue the games the team had won and lost in the last five years, the plays they'd run and how he would have done it, if he were coaching them. Halfway through her plate of ribs, Frankie's head was swimming with strategies and statistics.

"You must have been quite a ball player in school," she commented.

"I didn't play. My boy did, though. Cole was Port Arthur's star running back his whole varsity career. I never missed a game."

She could well imagine Pal at his son's football games. She pitied the poor child, not to mention his coaches. She was relieved when the waitress returned.

"Is everything all right over here? Can I get you anything?"

"You want another beer?" Pal asked.

"No, no thanks. One's my limit." She smiled at the waitress. "Everything's delicious. I'd like a glass of ice water, though, when you get a chance."

With his earlier line of conversation disrupted, Pal's talk

turned to his ex-wife, Candy, and all of her flaws. She was selfish. She wore too much make up. She couldn't cook a lick, not even hamburgers. Frankie counted to ten again, slowly. Oh, how she would have liked to have heard Candy's side of the story!

Her mind wandered to stain colors. She thought she had settled on mahogany for her living room floor, but she'd picked up a color wheel at Cunningham's Hardware Store, and now she was having trouble deciding. The mahogany was both classic and classy, but the gray-blue colonial went so nicely with the walls. Maybe she would buy a sample of each color, try before you buy, as the saying went … Her mind snapped back to the conversation when she realized Pal was talking about Tracy.

"She messed me up tough, running off like she did. I couldn't eat, couldn't sleep. I ended up losing my job at General Foods and that's when Tracy hired me on. That was more than six years ago. Now he couldn't run the place without me. "

"Really?" She sipped her water. "He told you that?"

"Not in so many words. But Tracy, he's not really that organized. I keep the business running smooth and he knows it."

"Have you known each other a long time?"

"Since high school. We were all in the same grade together, me and Candy and Tracy and Joanne. We even used to double date sometimes."

The words caused a pinprick in her heart. Tracy and his wife had been together for almost their entire lives. She couldn't imagine a love that comfortable and enduring.

Pal guzzled down his beer and signaled the waitress for another. "In fact our boys were born a month apart. My Cole works for Tracy in the summers. He's got one more year at Shawnee State."

"I didn't know Tracy had a son. Does he work for his dad, too?"

"Lord no, not anymore. Dalton, he's kind of a mess."

The waitress returned with Pal's beer. He took a swallow, picking up where he'd left off. "We did everything together. 'Course Tracy and Jo stayed married, whereas Candy and me, well, didn't. I kind of stopped hanging out with them after Candy left me. It was too awkward, since Candy and Jo were still friends. And then after Jo passed, Tracy didn't want to do much of anything anymore. Except work." He took another swallow of beer. "He still doesn't."

His words went through her like a lightning bolt. It took her a moment to process them. "She died?" she asked casually. "Tracy's wife?"

"Yup. Probably been four or five years, by now. Between you and me? He's just not that much fun anymore."

Her heart started pounding foolishly. "What happened to her?"

"Cancer. Some female kind, I think. She didn't last too long after they found out. By the time she got diagnosed, it was already too late."

Frankie's head was spinning again. Tracy Johanson was a widower? That changed everything.

Pal swallowed the last of his beer. "So do you want to go dancing or anything?"

No, she did not want to go dancing with Pal. She wanted to throw her arms open wide and dance for joy beneath the stars. As far as she was concerned, this date was over!

"Actually Pal, I have a little bit of a headache. Would you mind just taking me home?"

"Sure thing. It's all the smoke in here from the grills. If it was me, I'd install better vent fans. I'll go and pay the bill and then we can take off." He opened his wallet and leafed through it. "You mind leaving the tip?"

She'd thought saying she had a headache would make him drop her off and go away, but when they reached her house, he followed her onto the porch.

"You mind if I use your bathroom?"

She showed him where it was and returned to the living room. Maybe if she waited by the door he'd get the hint. After a few moments he returned and sat down on her couch, clearly ready for more conversation. By then her head really did ache. She thought of Lilly's suggestion of telling him to get out of town, but she couldn't bring herself to be that rude.

"Would you like a cup of coffee?" she asked.

"Sure."

She made the coffee, carried it to the living room, and handed it to him. He was flipping through her meager collection of CDs. "Matchbox Twenty, huh?"

"Do you like them?"

"Not so much." He shrugged. "Candy used to love them. I took her to see Rob Thomas once. He was okay. If it was me, I'd have played a little longer though and given people their money's worth."

"Of course you would have," she murmured.

She heard a soft mewling behind the guest room door and jumped up. "Oh gosh, I'd better check on my boys."

His coffee cup stopped halfway to his lips. "Boys?"

She opened the door and Nutmeg bolted out with Pepper close on his heels.

"You've got cats?" Pal squealed.

Before she could grab them, they scrambled up his pant legs and hopped onto his shoulders. He swatted at them, spilling his coffee in his lap. "I didn't know you had cats!"

His look of absolute horror made her want to giggle and she bit the inside of her cheek. "Just these two, for now. But I'm going to be starting up a cat rescue soon, so I'll have at least five or six more." It was only an idea she toyed with, nothing she actually intended to do, and she was amazed at how smoothly the words slid from her lips.

"*A-choo!* I'm allergic to cats."

"Oh, dear."

Pepper climbed back up his leg.

"*A-choo!*" He slapped his coffee cup down on the end table, grabbed the kitten and all but threw it at her. "I've got to go."

He jumped to his feet and bolted out the door without another word.

She stared after him, openmouthed, as the door slammed behind him. The kittens also stared after him, as if they, too, were unsure what had just happened.

"You naughty boys," she said softly. She scooped them up in her arms and hugged them. "Oh, you dear, sweet, naughty little boys!"

The giggles broke free then, and for the second time in

seven months, she laughed until she cried.

Part Two
Rivers in the Desert

Chapter Six

The next morning Frankie walked into Saint Bridgette's with a spring in her step and a song in her heart. She'd awakened with a curious sense of optimism and she was determined to look for the positives in her new church.

She was happy to see that there were more people in attendance this week. They stood clustered inside the vestibule, chatting with each other. Not one of them acknowledged her as she walked past. She might as well have been invisible. But she would not let that bother her. Maybe it took people a few weeks to accept a newcomer. She'd gone to Saint Sebastian's for so long it was hard to remember a time when she was new there.

She only hoped she'd never made anyone feel unwelcome. She slid into the same pew as the week before and opened her bulletin. This week's message was entitled Rivers in the Desert. She'd gotten a lot out of Father Joe's homily last week and she was eager to hear what he would say today.

The organ played an unfamiliar hymn that seemed sweet and beautiful. As the song played, two young blonde girls walked up the aisle and lit the candles on the altar. She found it incredible how much things had changed over the years. She'd been a churchgoer all her life, sitting between her mother and father Sunday after Sunday in the unpadded church pew at St. Sebastian's.

Oh, how she'd wanted to be a server, to ring the bells and light the candles and wear one of the beautiful white robes. But it was strictly a boy thing, in those days.

The rites and prayers were comforting in their familiarity.

When the reader stepped up to the ambo to give the first reading, she gave him her full attention.

"Today's reading is from the book of Isaiah, Chapter forty-three, verses eighteen and nineteen. 'Do not remember the former things, nor consider the things of old. Behold I will do a new thing. Now it shall spring forth; shall you not know it? I will even make a road in the wilderness and rivers in the desert.' This is the Word of the Lord."

"Thanks be to God."

The reading startled her with its relevance. She fished a pen out of her purse and underlined the chapter and verse in her bulletin. She'd have to go home and read that again, in private, where she could ponder its meaning. She was so intent on the first reading that she missed the second reading altogether.

Once again, Father Joe's homily did not disappoint. He talked about giving God your desert places, your failures and your disappointments, and allowing him to give your soul refreshing rivers in their place. She sat in her pew, stunned.

How did Father Joe do that? How did he look inside her soul like that and find just the words she needed to hear? She felt like she'd been walking through a desert for months, not a drop of water in sight. But things were changing now, she could feel it deep inside herself. Maybe she'd come through the hot, parched deserts of her life, and had refreshing springs to look forward to.

It was sixteen days after Alonzo's funeral that she got called into the principal's office at St. Sebastian's Elementary School. Sal DeFranco sat behind his desk, his hands folded in front of him.

"Come on in," he said solemnly, clearly not himself.

"Am I in trouble?" she asked, grinning.

"Frankie, have a seat."

His tone worried her and she sank into a chair.

"I hate to have to tell you this, especially so soon after Alonzo's death."

"Sal, you're scaring me."

"We've lost our funding, Frankie. We're going to have to close St. Sebastian's."

Tears sprang to her eyes. "No. How…?"

"We've been struggling for two years, now. The building's falling apart. I'm sure you've noticed how badly our enrollment has dropped. We've tried everything to keep the school afloat, but it's just not enough. The Diocese doesn't feel it's worth it to keep the doors open any longer. I'm so sorry."

"How soon will we be closing?"

"We'll be open until Christmas. After break, St. Paul's will take on our sixty-five students. I want you to know that I went to bat for all of you. But I'm afraid they're already fully staffed."

She nodded, overcome by feelings of grief and loss that losing Alonzo could not even compare to.

"I'm going to do everything I can to help you," he said. "After all, we've always been in this together, haven't we?"

It was Sal DeFranco who had hired her almost thirty years before. It was his first year as principal of the school and he'd liked her enough to take a chance on her. He'd hired her to oversee the school lunch program, to plan and cook the meals even though she had no formal education or experience.

"I know some people. I'm going to start making some calls."

A week later, she met with him again. "I have good news for you this time," he said. "I contacted an old friend of mine, Tony Argenteri. He's the principal at Holy Child Academy down in Port Arthur. It seems he's losing not only his assistant principal next year, but his food service director as well. As they say, you're in like Flynn." He sat back, a broad smile on his face.

Move away from Cincinnati? Start a whole new life, somewhere else? It was too much to take in. The implications terrified her and her first reaction was to refuse. "I can't move to Port Arthur, Sal. And I certainly can't commute an hour and a half both ways every day. But thank you so much for doing that for me."

"Promise me you'll at least give it some thought, Frankie. Go for an interview, look around. I don't know much about Port Arthur, but Holy Child is a good, solid school and Tony is willing to hire you for next school year on my recommendation. The interview would only be a formality."

"I'll think about it," she told him, though she had no intention of doing any such thing.

She updated her resume and started applying for food service positions at schools, hospitals, and nursing homes, places that offered decent wages and along with benefit packages. Every application was met with rejection. Lowering her expectations, she tried restaurants and supermarket bakeries.

Desperate, she even applied for a deli position at a mini-gas-mart. It seemed that no one would have her. She'd heard that unemployment was skyrocketing and that jobs were scarce, but she never really understood how competitive the job market was until it was her that didn't have one.

After six weeks of applying for jobs and being rejected, it became painfully clear that good jobs were nonexistent for fifty- year-old women with no college education. She consented to an interview at Holy Child in January, after St. Sebastian's School was shuttered. As Sal had promised, she was hired on the spot. She breathed an uneasy sigh of relief.

Whether she would enjoy her new position or not was still a question mark that hung in the air above her. But now she thought that maybe it would turn out to be a river in the desert. At the very least, it would be better than no job at all.

After church she made a cup of coffee and carried it out to her porch. She scanned the length of the sidewalk, hoping that Lilly would come by. Fifteen minutes later her friend materialized, her canvas shopping bag slung over her shoulder.

"No wagon today?" Frankie asked.

"I don't scrap on Sundays," Lilly said, climbing onto the porch. "I just came by to see how it went last night with Wayne Wrong. And to see if you have any more of them cookies." Her eyes skimmed over Frankie's dress. "Ooh girl, don't you look nice. You're not expecting gentleman company, are you?"

"No, definitely not. These are my church clothes. Oh, Lilly, wait until I tell you about my date!"

Over a second cup of coffee and a plate of biscotti, she told Lilly all of the grizzly details, ending with the debacle with the kittens.

Lilly cackled and slapped her knee. "Lord have mercy, it

serves him right. Can you leave the tip, indeed. What kind of decent man does that?"

She thought of telling Lilly about Tracy, and what she'd found out last night, but then thought better of it. Lilly was the best friend she'd had in a long, long time. She already loved her dearly, but maybe Tracy was something she would keep to herself for a while.

"Lilly, do you believe that God makes rivers in the desert? I mean, do you think he lets us go through hard times so we can appreciate the good times when he sends them? Or do you think everything is just random coincidence?"

"Honey, if I didn't believe the Good Lord had a reason for all I've been through, I'd lay right down and die."

"Me too."

Lilly looked as though she might say more, but then didn't.

•

By Monday evening Frankie's emotions were engaged in a full- fledged tug-of-war. She wanted to see Tracy as badly as she didn't want to see Pal. She'd read an online article: *So You've Met the Man of Your Dreams! Here Are Twenty Five Foolproof Ways To Reel Him In!*

Though silly, the article had given her some good ideas she wanted to try out on Tracy. She only hoped she wouldn't scoop Pal up in her net, as well. If the man had any lingering illusions of starting a relationship with her, even after his disastrous encounter with Pepper and Nutmeg, she'd have to put them to rest. And that was something she didn't look forward to. When the pickup truck pulled up in front of her house that evening she was delighted to see that Tracy was alone.

"Working alone tonight?" she asked.

"Pal's sick. Or so he says," he grumbled. "He took off about an hour ago like his pants were on fire." He shrugged. "I can finish it by myself."

Hiding a smile, she stuck her hands in her back pockets. Tip number twelve had been Be Agreeable: Offer to help in any way you can.

"I can help paint, if you want me to."

He seemed surprised, but not unpleasantly. "All right, if you don't mind. You can start the posts while I fill in the nail holes."

She went inside to change into her old clothes. When she returned, he was dabbing putty into the nail holes. She opened the can of paint he'd set out for her and went to work on the posts. They worked without speaking, and she was trying to think of a clever conversation starter when he asked, "How was your date?"

She slid her brush along the post, not looking at him. "It was pretty much a disaster."

He stopped working and faced her. "How so?"

"I guess he didn't like my cats."

He snorted and turned away again.

They worked for the next hour and a half, saying little more. When the porch was finally finished, she stood back to admire their work. The porch was gorgeous.

"I can't thank you enough, Tracy. I love this. The columns are perfect."

"The style works well here. I'm pleasantly surprised, myself."

"Let me go and get your money. Is a check okay?"

"A check will be fine."

She went inside and retrieved the check she'd written earlier that day. When she handed it to him, he stuck it in his pocket. "I'll get back to you in a week or two about those other jobs."

"Okay." There was a long pause, and everything inside her urged her to make the first move and ask him out.

She couldn't do it. She watched as he got in his truck and drove away, swallowing her disappointment. A week or two? Why so long?

Her rational mind told her he was a busy man. Hadn't he said his schedule was jammed? She could hardly expect him to clear his calendar just because she couldn't see out her kitchen window. She would get through the two weeks, somehow. After all, she'd survived for fifty years without his company. But knowing he was available made it that much harder to wait.

She thought again of Father Joe's homily. Her life with

Alonzo had been a desert wasteland. She started out her marriage with dreams of a loving home and husband. Of the children they would create, and the lifetime of companionship they'd share along the way. Was that too much to want?

Evidently so. Instead of feeling cherished, she'd often felt lonely. She'd been afraid of Alonzo's mood swings, and crushed by his criticism. She'd cried herself to sleep for too many nights, feeling unloved and unlovely. Did she dare to hope that her dream could still come true? Would God take pity on her and send rain to heal and nourish her parched spirit?

•

So the date with Pal had been a disaster. Why wasn't Tracy surprised? And why did knowing that make him feel so satisfied? As much as he'd like to, he wouldn't ask Frankie out. Last week had made him see that he'd been right all along. He was better off alone. No drama. No headaches. No stomachaches.

No companionship? No evenings spent in the company of a beautiful woman? An inner voice challenged.

He sighed. When he'd married Joanne, he thought all of this was behind him. He had their future all mapped out. They would raise their child, retire early, maybe buy the RV Joanne always wanted and travel cross country. They were supposed to grow old together. Growing old alone had never figured into his plan.

He'd known so much disappointment in the past few years and sustained so many losses. He couldn't go there again. Another dose of disappointment would be the end of him. As much as he liked her, he would keep Frankie Bonetti at arm's length. It would be better for him in the long run.

Chapter Seven

The next morning Frankie put her old clothes back on. She'd decided to go with the mahogany stain after all and she was anxious to get started. It would be a messy project. She'd have to use the back door for a few days, and keep the kittens sequestered in the kitchen, but now that she'd bought the stain she was anxious to finish the floor and now seemed as good a time as any.

The living room was small and the first coat of stain took no time at all to apply. She had opened all the windows and set up an oscillating fan to speed the drying time. With nothing to do but wait, she went out front to plant the impatiens and the hostas she'd bought at the Home Depot.

The soil out front was much more accommodating than what she'd encountered along the side of the house. With each new plant she put in the ground, the space came more alive. The flowers definitely added curb appeal.

Deciding to go one step further, she went back to Home Depot and bought six bags of rich, brown mulch and four big, leafy ferns to hang between the new porch posts.

Standing back to admire her work, she smiled. There. That was more like it. She'd have to get some better porch furniture, though. The plastic lawn chairs didn't exactly fit the look she was trying to create. Maybe she'd even hang a porch swing from the ceiling. But she'd done enough impulse shopping for the day.

The next time she saw Lilly, she would ask about a good second-hand store. Maybe she could find some inexpensive used furniture and paint it, or something.

By Friday afternoon she'd seen nothing of Lilly at all. That seemed strange to Frankie. She hadn't realized how much she relied on the other woman's company. Lilly was the only friend she had in Port Arthur, and without her, she had no way of keeping the loneliness at bay. Thank heavens she had her house to keep her busy until her new job started.

With two coats of stain and another of varnish, the floor looked beautiful beyond her wildest dreams. Her new curtains had arrived UPS earlier that morning, and she couldn't wait to hang them up.

She was in the kitchen ironing the first panel when she heard a knock at her back door. Thinking it might be Lilly, she hurried to open it. Rhoda stood on her deck, holding an enormous bouquet of mixed flowers.

"Rhoda, how are you? Come in!"

"I knocked at the front door, but I didn't get any answer, so I came around back. The porch looks fantastic, by the way."

Frankie searched the petite, blonde-haired, blue-eyed woman's face, looking for evidence that she was related to Tracy. She saw no resemblance.

"I'm super happy with the job Tracy did," she said. "Let me take those."

Rhoda handed her the bouquet. "Happy housewarming!" "Thank you so much. They're gorgeous! You didn't have to do that."

"I should have been here a week ago with them. I'm sorry to be so late. My daughter's been sick with a stomach bug and Guy is out of town. I've been running in circles for the last few days. I don't realize how much I rely on my husband until he isn't there." She glanced through the archway into the living room. "Oh my word, look at this room!" Walking through the archway, she gazed around in wonder. "Francesca, it looks amazing."

"Thank you."

"This doesn't even look like the same house. I can't believe you've done this much already."

"One room at a time."

The kittens had scampered away to hide when Rhoda knocked on the door, but finally their curiosity got the better of them and they came prowling out from under the table.

"Look at these two!" Rhoda lowered herself to a squat and stretched out her hand. "Here kitty, kitty."

"They'll shed all over your black pants," Frankie warned.

As if she hadn't heard, Rhoda picked Nutmeg up and stroked him behind the ears. "I just love kittens. I'd get one, but Sassy would have a fit."

Frankie smiled. "Who is Sassy?"

"My Yorkie. He's actually more the size of a cat than a dog, but he thinks he's a Rottweiler." She stood, still holding the kitten. "You've really got a flair for decorating, Francesca. Have you ever thought of doing it professionally?"

"Oh, no. I just do it for me. I'm not that good."

"Yes, you are. Trust me."

"Would you like something to drink? I have lemonade, or I could make coffee. It wouldn't take a minute."

"I wish I could. But I have a house to show in—" she checked her watch. "Actually, right now. I just wanted to drop the flowers off. And if you're free, I wanted to invite you to a Memorial Day picnic I'm having on Monday."

"Really?"

"It's nothing fancy, just a few friends. I thought it might be a nice chance for you to meet some people, make some friends."

"Let me think about it."

"Sure. Do you still have my number?"

"I have it memorized."

Rhoda laughed her deep, throaty laugh. "Great. Call me in a day or two. I'm thinking we'll throw some steaks on the grill, probably around three o'clock, after the parade. You're welcome to come to that with us, too, if you'd like. Every high school band in the county will be there, along with all of the fire trucks you can handle.

She chuckled. "I'll let you know."

"Great. Talk soon." She walked out the door, and then turned back. Grinning, she handed Frankie her kitten. "This is yours."

•

The weekend, at last. Tracy couldn't remember the last time he'd had a two-day weekend, let alone three. With back-to-back jobs, he'd been working from morning to night, seven days a week, for the past month.

Not that he was complaining. Work slowed down in the winter months and he relied on a steady spring and summer season to keep the company going.

Next week they would have to start a complete renovation on a house on Zanesville Drive, and finish up a roof on Parkview. He'd see if he could fit one of Frankie's projects in the week after that. Jace could probably handle the window by himself. That would still leave him five men to work on other projects.

Frankie.

It was astounding how often his thoughts returned to her. Alarming, really. It had taken him four years to get to where he was. To the point of being okay with being alone. And then she came along, making him want things he'd thought he could do without; candlelight dinners, quiet country drives, picnics by the lake. All of the things he'd shared with Joanne.

He walked into Luigi's and had just placed his order when his cell phone rang.

"Hey, Rho."

"Hey. What are you doing?"

"I'm sitting at Luigi's, waiting for a pizza. What are you doing?"

"I'm calling to remind my favorite brother about my picnic on Monday. It's Memorial Day, so I know you won't be working."

"I'll be there, Rhodie."

"And you'll come to the parade, too?"

He sighed. "I don't know. Probably not."

"Oh, but you have to come. Allie is twirling. Wait a minute, here she is."

"Hi, Uncle Tracy."

He smiled. How he adored his niece. He'd loved every minute of watching her evolve from a chubby baby, to a busy toddler, to a little girl who brought him bouquets of dandelions and jars full of lightning bugs. How was it possible that she'd so quickly become a lovely fourteen-year-old, all giggles and makeup and nail polish?

"Hey there, Allie Cat. Are you feeling better?"

"Finally. Are you coming to watch my parade on Monday?"

"I wouldn't miss it for the world, baby."

"Okay, thanks! I've missed a week of practices, though, so don't expect too much."

"I'm sure you'll do great."

"See you Monday. Love you, Uncle Tracy."

"Love you more."

"You still there?" Rhoda asked

"I'm here. But my pizza is ready, so I have to go now."

"You'll come watch Allie twirl, though?"

"Yes, I'll come watch Allie twirl."

"Great. And I'll need you to do the steaks, later. You know what a disaster Guy is when it comes to the grill."

"I'll see you Monday, Sis."

He ended the call, smiling. Thank God he had his family. Without them, he would feel disconnected from the world.

Chapter Eight

It was rare for Frankie to miss a Sunday service. Mass was something that had always been a part of her life. It was important to her, and besides that, her mother had taught her that not going to mass was a sin. She'd planned to run up to Cincinnati and decorate her parents' graves on Monday morning, but now that Rhoda had invited her to the party she would have to do it today. She hoped God would understand, just this once.

She'd gone to a local florist the day before and selected a beautiful pot of pink and white geraniums, her mother's favorites. The florist had mixed in baby's breath and trailing ivy and the arrangement was stunning. Pulling into the cemetery entrance, she cast a last glance into the back seat, thankful that the urn hadn't tipped over on the long drive over.

She retrieved the arrangement from the car and carried it, along with a small bouquet for Alonzo, across the grassy lawn to the familiar spot beneath the leafy old sugar maple. She'd been decorating her parents' grave for nearly twenty years.

She'd always heard that people's loved ones were still present in spirit, even after death. She didn't know whether she believed her parents were looking down on her from heaven or not. They hadn't been all that attentive when they walked the earth beside her and she doubted they would take an interest now. But dressing the grave seemed like her duty, and besides, it was the last thing she would ever be able to do for them.

Sacred Heart was an old cemetery, and it wasn't very well maintained, but it was where generations of Ragazzo's before her had been laid to rest. Finding the grave, she brushed away a scattering of last year's dried leaves from in front of the headstone and set the urn in place.

"Here I am again, Mom and Dad," she said. "I got the pink and white geraniums again this year. I hope you like them."

She'd never been one to linger in the cemetery, to sit by the grave site and pour out her heart. She hadn't had a lot to say to her parents when they were alive, and had even less to say to them now. She straightened the pot of flowers, made her way to the newer part of Sacred Heart, and dropped the bouquet on Alonzo's grave. This time she said nothing at all.

Her parents had been in their mid-forties when Frankie was born. They were fifteen years away from retirement and set in their ways and she'd always felt that she was a cross they'd had to bear. A disappointment. If she'd been a boy, there would have at least been someone to carry on the Ragazzo name, but she was a girl, and not a particularly pretty or athletic one, and definitely not very smart.

When she'd announced her decision to become an elementary school teacher, like her mother, they had both seemed so proud. She'd struggled through her first semester of college, and the rare approval she saw in their eyes had pushed her to keep going, despite the tears and frustration and endless nights of studying.

When her first semester grade list yielded a B, three Cs and a D, she'd stubbornly stuck with it. But when her second semester ended with three Cs and two Fs, she'd seen the disappointment in the firm set of her mother's mouth and simply given up.

That summer her mother had seen a help wanted ad in the paper and had pushed Frankie to apply at St. Sebastian's.

"You're not just going to mope around here, Francesca. You need to get out and get a job, earn some money so you can stand on your own two feet. Surely to goodness even you can cook sloppy joes and canned corn!"

The shame of her mother's words still stung, even after all these years.

Her mother and father had wholeheartedly supported her decision to marry Alonzo Bonetti. They were thrilled to be free of the responsibility of her, even though by then she'd been out on her own for nearly a decade. Within two years of her marriage they had died six months apart.

Leaving the cemetery, she took a left-hand turn. Instead of heading back to the highway, she continued through the residential area until she came to Sunny Dell Street. Driving slowly, she regarded her old neighborhood with curiosity. It had become more and more shabby as one by one, the old family homesteads were turned into rental properties.

Her childhood home looked abandoned, with its broken windows and untended lawn. She thought how horrified her mother would be at the chipping, bright blue paint and the faded bedsheets flapping in the broken windows. Sighing, she turned the car around and headed west. As long as she was taking a trip down Memory Lane, she may as well make one more detour.

She'd priced Alonzo's house to sell, and it had sold quickly. She drove past it now feeling no sadness, only mild curiosity. The new owners had added shutters and painted the front door cherry red. She'd always wanted to do that.

Alonzo had liked it brown. He'd argued that red would take away from the house's resale value, though they both knew he never intended to sell it. The red looked fabulous, but what did that matter to her now? She would take Father Joe's advice and not look back.

From now on, she was moving forward.

•

The next morning she awoke to cloudy skies and rain, but by noon the sun had come out. She opened her closet and took stock of her clothing. What would Rhoda wear? No doubt something ridiculously casual, and yet supremely stylish. Rhoda could wear a trash bag and make it look like the latest thing.

She decided on a pair of white capris, sandals, and a red-and-white striped top. In the bathroom, she discovered that the kittens had chewed up her toothbrush, so she used her finger instead. She worked some gel into her hair and fluffed it. As a last touch, she applied a coat of red lipstick and a spritz of Soft Musk perfume. She studied her reflection in the mirror. She'd never been a beauty, had always settled for passable, but some days were better than others. She felt like this was one of her better days.

She wasn't going to lie to herself. The extra care she took stemmed from the fact that Tracy would probably be there today. She was so looking forward to seeing him again.

At one o'clock she heard a knock at the door and opened it to find a man she didn't know.

"Hello?"

"Hi, Francesca?"

"Yes."

He grinned. "I'm Guy Swanson, Rhoda's husband. She's saving our spots at the parade, so she sent me to pick you up."

"Oh. Okay. I made some eggs. Let me go and get them."

He pointed at the chairs on the porch. "I'll grab one of these lawn chairs for you, if that's okay."

When she was settled into the passenger seat of his SUV, he smiled again. "So Rhoda tells me you're from Cincinnati. How do you like Port Arthur so far?"

Guy Swanson was beyond good-looking. He was the kind of good looking that her younger self could not even seem to talk in front of. But she was more mature now. A middle aged widow, with nothing to prove.

"I like it, I guess. It's kind of too soon to tell, since I haven't started my new job yet. I'll be starting at Holy Child Academy in August, and a job can make or break a place. But I like it just fine, so far. So far so good!" Oh, Lord. She was babbling.

"Cool."

"What do you do for a living, Guy?"

"I'm a sales rep for a furniture company."

"That sounds like it must be interesting work."

He shrugged. "It keeps my wife in new furniture and I get to meet a lot of people, so it's all good." Main Street was blocked off, so he swung the SUV into an alley. "This is probably as close as we're going to get."

They walked down Main Street, Guy carrying her chair for her. The two-hundred-year-old business district, though tired, was not without its charm. The buildings were mostly red or whitewashed brick, with contrasting colors of trim. Oversized baskets of flowers hung from the old gas lamp posts that lined the brick street. She noticed a couple of cute shops she hadn't seen before and made a mental note to come back and check them out sometime.

In the center of Main Street was the town square, a lovely green spot with benches and trees and a large gazebo where she'd been told there was live music on summer evenings. Today it was set up as a judge's booth and surrounded by people in folding chairs. Port Arthur had twenty thousand residents, and it looked to Frankie like every one of them had turned out for the parade.

"Guy! Over here!"

Scanning the crowd, Frankie saw Rhoda waving to them. Threading their way through the crowd, they walked over to where she sat.

Guy set her lawn chair beside an empty one and slid into the chair next to Rhoda's. Moments later, Rhoda waved again and Frankie looked to see Tracy walking toward them. Her heart leapt like a pony.

As he drew closer, his glance raked over her. The pointed glance he shot his sister was not lost on her. He obviously hadn't known she would be there today.

"Hey stranger," Rhoda greeted him. "You made it, and on time, too!"

"Hey Rhodie, Guy. Hello Frankie."

"Hi Tracy."

He sat in the empty chair next to hers. His nearness was intoxicating, though she could feel tension coming off of him in waves. She couldn't help noticing the amicable way in which he and Guy chatted while they waited for the parade to begin.

So it must have been her that was stressing him out. Had she done something wrong? She tried to think back to the last time she'd seen him. Her thoughts were interrupted as the first band approached the judge's stand.

"First up is the pride of Port Arthur," the announcer's voice boomed across the square, "The one, the only, Port Arthur Marching Mustangs!"

The band played wonderfully and the crowd was generous with its applause. After that there were Boy and Girl Scout troops and elementary school floats and Port Arthur's fire department. Then two more local high school bands. As a new band approached, her group applauded wildly. Rhoda hurried close to the street, iPhone in hand.

"Next up we have Port Arthur's very own John Glenn Middle School Marching Mustangs," the announcer boomed.

The band played and behind it came the color guard, and then the majorettes. Guy and Tracy stood to their feet, cheering wildly as a squad of girls in a sparkling red costumes pranced past, twirling their batons. The one on the end, a pretty blonde, shot Rhoda a nervous glance before her gaze swept the crowd. When it fell on Guy, she smiled. Obviously this was their daughter. She threw her baton high in the air, and Frankie winced as it dropped back to the ground. The girl scooped it up and kept going.

"That's all right, baby girl, you got this!" Guy shouted.

Tracy leaned in close to her. "That's my niece, Allie."

"She's beautiful!"

Rhoda returned to them. "I suppose she'll make me delete the video now. She gets so upset when she makes a mistake."

"She's an overachiever," Tracy said. "Like someone else I know."

There were more floats, more bands, and more fire trucks than Frankie had ever seen in one place. The parade lasted a full hour and a half and she couldn't remember when she'd enjoyed a parade more.

•

As the crowd began to thin, Allie joined them. "Well, I messed that up."

Tracy scooped her up in bear hug. "You did fine. And you were the prettiest girl in the parade."

"You're just saying that because you're my uncle," she said, but the compliment obviously pleased her. "Mom, you didn't post that video did you?"

"No, Allie."

"Good. Please delete it."

"I already did."

"Can we go home? I'm starving."

They threaded through the crowd and made their way down Main Street, Allie's arm linked through Tracy's. "Can I ride home with you, Uncle Tracy?"

"I thought you'd never ask."

Frankie rode in the back of Guy and Rhoda's SUV. She looked out the window, catching random snippets of their conversation. "I wish the outfits weren't quite so skimpy," Guy grumbled.

"Majorette uniforms have been skimpy ever since there were majorettes. If you remember, dear, I wore one myself, a hundred years ago."

"And I didn't like it any better then than I do now."

"Liar!"

Within a few minutes they pulled into the driveway of a charming three-color Victorian home. Its base color was a mossy green, with the front door painted dusty rose, and the porch spindles and shutters done in cream.

"This is gorgeous, Rhoda. It looks just like something you'd see in a magazine."

"See?" Guy gave his wife an affectionate shove. "We've only lived in this one two years, and already she's tired of it. She falls in love with every house she sees and wants me to buy it for her. It ain't easy being married to a realtor." But his admiration for her was obvious.

Tracy and Allie pulled in behind them, followed by a dust-covered, blue minivan. Frankie watched as the doors opened and a family of six spilled out.

"I'm so glad you could come," Rhoda said, kissing the woman on the cheek. "Francesca, this is Guy's brother, Johnny, and his gorgeous wife, Jasmine. And I think some of these kids are theirs. "

"All of these, and more," said Jasmine, patting her bulging abdomen.

The teens and tweens immediately ran off to the back yard. While the adults stood talking in the driveway, Frankie admired the tea roses and the hibiscus in Rhoda's flower beds.

"Would you like to see the house?" Rhoda asked.

"I'd love to."

Rhoda led her to the kitchen, which had a modern, industrial flair and all of the latest gadgets. She stowed the deviled eggs Frankie'd brought in the stainless steel fridge and then led her into the living room. "I've done quite a bit of research on Victorian homes. This would have been a formal parlor, back in the day. I'm really not sure what I want to do with it yet. Any suggestions?"

It looked perfect to Frankie as it was, with its crown molding and its pocket doors and pure white furniture. Rhoda was looking at her expectantly, but how could she explain? The reason she knew what to do in her house was that somehow, the house told her what to do. She was that in tune with her home. But that would sound crazy.

"Let me give it some thought," she said.

By the time they got outside, Tracy was manning the grill. A few more people had arrived and they stood chatting in groups while the kids splashed raucously in the in-ground swimming pool.

When the food was ready, Frankie took her plate to one of the glass-topped tables that surrounded the pool. She tried to keep up with the conversation around her, but soon felt lost. And left out. These people had known each other all their lives. They knew all of the same people and hung out at the same places. She was an outsider. Maybe it had been a mistake to come. If only Tracy would talk to her…

After lunch, she rolled up the legs of her capris and went to sit by the pool. She smiled as she watched the kids play. She'd never had a lot of friends. Her parents hadn't wanted kids underfoot, and her cousins were all much older than she was.

She would have loved to have been a part of a big, family gathering like this. The thought made her feel lonely, and she was contemplating making an excuse and going home when she saw the cousins gather around the pool filter. She had spent enough time around kids at St. Sebastian's to know they were up to something.

Suddenly Allie squealed. "Uncle Tracy, there's a snake in

the filter!"

"Is it alive?" he asked, already making his way over.

"I don't know. I can't tell."

"Don't touch it!" Rhoda shouted.

"Kids, get away from that snake," Jasmine hollered.

Tracy reached the group, squatted beside the filter, and squinted inside. "I don't see any—"

Frankie saw it coming but was too surprised to cry out as Allie and one of the larger boys got behind Tracy and shoved him into the pool.

Laughter erupted all around as Tracy came up sputtering. "Oh, someone's gonna pay for that … Allie!"

She ran off shrieking as he climbed from the pool.

Rhoda was nearly doubled over with laughter. "You have to admit, Tracy, she got you good."

"You liked that, did you?"

"Yes. I did."

He walked over to her, scooped her up, and threw her over his shoulder.

"You wouldn't dare!" she shrieked.

"I wouldn't? You forget who you're talking to, sister."

"Tracy, put me down! Guy! Do something!"

"I am doing something," he said, tipping his beer to his lips. Tracy carried his sister to the side of the pool and dumped her in. After that, chaos ensued as the party became an all-out water war. Everywhere she looked there were hoses spraying and buckets of water flying.

As she scrambled away from the side of the pool, one of the boys dumped a bucket of water over her head. The water was shockingly cold against her skin and she laughed so hard she couldn't catch her breath. Within moments all of the kids and most of the adults were in the pool.

"As long as we're in," Guy shouted, "we might as well play volleyball. Allie, go get the ball!"

It was a free-for-all, with women against men. Frankie didn't know the rules, but she soon discovered there weren't any anyway. They laughed and played like children, and as allegiances were formed, she felt her earlier loneliness melting away.

Eventually the game broke up and people drifted back to the tables. Tracy plopped himself down in the chair beside hers. "Aren't you glad you came?"

She grinned. "Absolutely!"

"I guess when Rhoda invited you she left out one small detail. Our family is nuts."

"I was an only child. I've never had this." She waved her arm in a gesture that encompassed the trashed pool area. "I loved it."

"Mom! I can't find my phone!" Allie shouted.

"Well you'd better find it! That's the second one I've bought you this year."

A Straight Talk phone sat on the table, its case decorated with glittery pink zebra stripes. Tracy picked it up. "Hello? Allie who?"

Allie came rushing over. "Give it to me, Uncle Tracy."

"I'm sorry, who is this? Dylan O'Brien? You want her to make a movie with you? Sorry, dude, I don't think she'd be interested in anything like that."

"Very funny," Allie said. She grabbed the phone from his hand and stalked away. Jasmine stood. "Come on, Jimmy. Let's gather up our soggy children and head home. This mama's tired. It was great meeting you, Frankie. We should have lunch sometime, you, me and Rhoda."

"I'd like that."

Tracy found a dry towel and wrapped it around her shoulders. "You're shivering."

"It got cold once the sun started to go down."

"Yeah, it's getting late and I have an early day tomorrow. Guess I should head out, too." He hesitated a beat, then asked, "Do you need a ride?"

In his truck, he turned up the heat. They warmed their icy fingers in front of the vent. "Oh yeah, that's the stuff," he said.

"I can't remember when I've enjoyed a day more," Frankie said, adding, "Your niece is adorable."

"Allie's a good girl. I worry, though. Kids have it tough today, a lot of crazy stuff going on that we didn't have to deal with, back in the day. I'll breathe easier when she's out of high school. Scratch that. I'll breathe easier when she's thirty."

"It's got to be hard, raising children these days. I never had any of my own, but I grew very attached to the kids at the school where I worked. I assume your kids are all grown up?"

He paused for a beat, then said, "I don't have any kids."

The statement puzzled her. She was sure Pal had said something about a boy. But she certainly wasn't going to question him, not now, when the ice was finally broken again between them. She stayed quiet as they drove through town. When he pulled up in front of her house, he let the truck idle.

"I have a crazy week coming up," he said. "But I'm thinking I can probably get at least one of your projects done after this week. "

"Oh, okay."

"I'll call you near the end of the week and let you know for sure."

"Sounds good."

"Okay then. Goodnight."

"Goodnight."

He idled at the curb until she slid her key in the lock and went inside.

Chapter Nine

If the heavens held back their rain in consideration of the Memorial Day holiday on Monday, they made up for it on Tuesday. It came down in torrents all morning, pounding like gunfire on Frankie's metal roof. She slept until ten o'clock, and lingered over a second cup of coffee, watching the rivers of water race down the street and pool in her back yard. So much for her plans.

She'd intended to spend the day working in her yard, had thought maybe she'd dig up a small plot near the back deck and plant the cottage garden Lilly had suggested. That plan was pretty well squashed now.

Most of the rooms in her house still needed to be painted, but she didn't have any more paint brushes, and she certainly wasn't going to venture to the hardware store in this kind of weather. The house would have to wait. Maybe she would treat herself to a pajama day and open one of the books she'd bought at the library's book sale several months ago.

She opened the cabinet in her living room and was perusing her stack of unread books when she heard a soft knock at the door. Puzzled, she went to open it. She wasn't expecting anything from UPS and who else in their right mind would come out on a day like this? Opening the door, she saw a bedraggled Lilly standing on her porch.

"Lilly, for goodness sakes, come in!" She stepped aside and hustled her friend into the living room. "What are you doing out in this weather?"

"I came by to see if you had any cough syrup I could have. I got a terrible cold."

"I'm sure I do. But if not I'll go and get some." Her glance moved over Lilly's glassy eyes and pale face, taking in the bright spots of color standing on her cheeks. "You don't look good at all."

"I'll be okay soon's I get something for this—" She broke off in a ragged fit of coughing that seemed to come from deep down in her lungs.

"Lilly, that's more than just a cold. How long have you been sick?"

"I don't know. A week, maybe."

"We need to get you to a doctor."

"I don't have no doctor."

"Urgent Care, then."

Lilly waved the words away as she struggled to catch her breath. "I don't have no insurance."

"You don't need insurance for Urgent Care. I think it costs like thirty-five dollars to be seen."

"It don't matter if it's five dollars, Frankie. I don't have it."

"Well I do."

"No."

"I'm not taking no for an answer. We're going to Urgent Care. But first we have to get you out of those wet clothes."

Before Lilly could protest further, Frankie hurried to her bedroom and opened the closet doors. She tore off her pajamas and pulled on a pair of jeans and a hoodie, then flipped through the hangers looking for something suitable for Lilly. She was a good twenty pounds heavier than her friend. What could she give her to wear? She pulled out a pair of joggers with a draw string waist and a matching sweatshirt and carried them back to the living room. "You'll be lost in these, but at least they're dry."

She helped Lilly into the clothes and rounded up a raincoat. "Here, put this on too."

She remembered seeing an Urgent Care center in a nearby plaza, so she headed that way. She had to take it slow. Her tires were having trouble gripping the waterlogged streets and her windshield wipers slashed furiously at the rain pouring down the windshield. It was a stressful few blocks, but at last they arrived.

She was glad to see that the waiting room was empty. She settled Lilly in a chair, and then went up to the reception desk.

"Your name?" a bored looking girl behind the desk asked.

"It's not me that needs to be seen. It's my friend over there. She has a terrible cough, and probably a fever."

"I'll need to see her ID."

She returned to Lilly and asked for her driver's license.

"I don't have no license."

"Do you have any type of ID card at all?"

"No."

Frustrated, Frankie returned to the window. "She doesn't have any ID on her."

"Then she can't be seen."

"But she's sick. She's very sick."

"I'm sorry," the girl said, not looking sorry at all.

Frankie thought she'd cry. Did nobody have any compassion anymore? What had society come to when a sick person could not be seen by a doctor because of a formality? "Fine." She slapped her license down on the counter. "Here's my ID. I'd like to be seen as soon as possible."

"Insurance card?"

"It'll be self-pay."

"It's thirty eight dollars and I'll need the money before you leave."

"Fine. Can we please see the doctor now?"

"Have a seat. The nurse practitioner will see you as soon as she's free."

She returned to Lilly and sat down beside her. Picking up a magazine, she flipped through it without looking at the pages. They were the only people here. What was taking so long? Finally the door opened and a middle-aged woman appeared.

"Frankie Bonetti?"

Frankie grabbed Lilly's hand and pulled her to her feet. "Come on, Frankie. They can see you now."

The nurse took Lilly's vital signs and her temperature. "You're running a fever," she announced. She moved her stethoscope around on Lilly's back and chest. "Take a few deep breaths for me. Ooh, that doesn't sound good. How long have you had that cough?"

"About a week."

She checked Lilly's eyes, nose and throat and asked her a few more questions. Finally she sat back on her stool. "Ms. Bonetti, you have bronchitis and a very bad sinus infection. I'm going to prescribe some antibiotics. Are you allergic to anything?"

"I don't think so," Lilly wheezed.

"I'm also going to phone in an inhaler and something for congestion. What pharmacy do you use?"

"I don't—"

"Call it in to Flack's," Frankie interjected, remembering the small drug store near her house.

"Drink lots and lots of water," the nurse said. "And try not to overdo it for the next couple of days."

Frankie paid the bill and then helped Lilly to the car.

"I'll pay it back," Lilly told her. "Might take me all summer, but I'll make it right with you."

Frankie knew money was a touchy subject with Lilly, so she merely nodded. When she reached the pharmacy, she told Lilly to wait in the car. "There's no sense in you getting soaked again. I'll just run in and get the medicine."

She picked up a couple of bottles of ginger ale, a half-gallon of ice cream, and a few cans of soup. With the grocery items and the prescriptions, the bill came to one hundred-fifty dollars and she was glad she'd had Lilly wait in the car. There was no point in her stressing over money when she could barely breathe.

On the short drive home, Frankie pondered how she might be able to convince her friend to stay the night. If Lilly did have anyone at home, they certainly hadn't kept a very good eye on her.

She pulled into the driveway and turned off the car. "Let's get inside and get a dose of medicine in you," she said.

In the kitchen, she poured Lilly a glass of water and shook two of the antibiotics and the decongestant into her hand. She gave them to her friend.

Lilly glanced out at the pouring rain. "I'll stay until the rain lets up a little, if you don't mind."

"Actually, Lilly, I was hoping you'd stay the night. I'd feel so

much better with you here. At least I'd know you were okay."
She saw relief pool in Lilly's eyes. "I won't lie to you, Frankie,
I wouldn't mind lying down for a little while."

She showed Lilly where the bathroom was and then settled
her into the guest room bed. When she returned with a glass of
water and a box of tissues, Lilly was sound asleep, the kittens
curled up at her side.

Under Frankie's watchful eye, Lilly slept all day and
through the night, waking only to take her medicines.

The next morning when Frankie awoke, the rain had
stopped. She looked in on Lilly and found her still sleeping.
She padded to the kitchen and started a pot of coffee. She'd just
poured her first cup when Lilly appeared.

"Good morning."

"Morning, Frankie."

"You look a little more rested." She got up and retrieved
Lilly's morning doses of medicine, poured a glass of water,
and handed them to Lilly. "Do you feel any better?"

"Some," she said, swallowing the pills.

"Do you feel like coffee?"

"Lord, no!"

"How about some toast?"

"I wouldn't turn it down."

She made them each two slices, got out a jar of jelly and
some butter, and set them on the table. Lily inhaled hers as if
she hadn't eaten in a month. She looked at Frankie, a sly smile
on her face.

"What?"

"I was just thinking about you and that ol' sourpuss at the
doctor's office. Girl, you got you some spunk." She took a sip
of water. "Will the real Frankie Bonetti please stand up, hah!"

They both laughed, and Lilly started coughing. "I guess I
should find my clothes and get on home."

"Actually, why don't you stay another day? It would be
nice to have someone to hang out with. Maybe I'll go and see if
there's anything decent in the Red Box."

Lilly regarded her for a long moment. "Why are you doing
this?"

"What?"

"Taking me to the doctor, giving up your room for me. Why?"

"Because you're my friend."

"You're a river in the desert, Frankie Bonetti," she said softly.

"Don't you have anyone at home, Lilly?" she asked gently. "Anyone to watch out for you?"

Lilly sighed. "No, I don't. My kids are scattered all around. They don't have much to do with their old mother no more. I s'pose they can't forgive me for staying with their father all those years."

"Was he abusive?"

"Meaner than a snake. He'd beat me silly for looking at him wrong. Never laid a hand on my kids. He'd rather to beat them up emotionally."

"I'm so sorry."

"Life goes on." She shrugged. "You do the best you can."

While Lilly was in the shower, Frankie went to the supermarket. She returned with three movies and found Lilly sitting on the couch, dressed in the nightgown Frankie had set out for her and playing with the kittens.

If Lilly hadn't been sick, it would have been a perfect day. They cried over silly movies and talked as if they'd been friends for years. She told Lilly about the Memorial Day picnic, and a little bit about Tracy.

"Who is this Mister Right you found you? Girl, whoever he is, he's got you glowing like a neon sign."

"I am not!"

"Mmmm, I know a glow when I'm looking at one. You in l-o-v-e love."

Frankie turned serious. "I don't know about love, but I'm in serious infatuation. It's kind of scary."

"Why's it scary?"

"Because I always manage to mess things up. I'm afraid I'll find a way to ruin it before it even gets started."

"Maybe you'll mess up and maybe you won't. That's a chance you got to take. Maybe he'll turn out to be your river."

She smiled. "Maybe."

As if talking about him had somehow summoned him, her

cell phone rang. She glanced at the screen in disbelief. "It's him!"

"No way."

"Hello?"

"Hi, Frankie. Hey listen, I think I can get at that window of yours on Monday for sure. Would five thirty work for you?"

"That would work just fine."

"Okay, I'll see you on Monday then. Unless…"

"Unless?"

"Would you be free to have dinner with me tonight?"

Her heart sank straight down to her toes. She'd waited for this invitation from the day she'd met Tracy Johanson. If it was any other day at all …

God, help me not to be selfish…

Aware of Lilly's eyes on her, she forced a note of cheerfulness into her voice. "I'd really love that, Tracy, but can we do it another time? I've got company today."

Lily started gesturing wildly but Frankie ignored her.

"Oh. Okay. Sure."

When she ended the call, Lilly glared at her. "Now why did you go and do that? He asked you for a date, didn't he?"

She smiled. "It's called playing hard to get, Lilly. It's the oldest trick in the book."

•

One step up and two steps back.

Tracy disconnected the call, feeling more than a little let down. Like a timid adolescent, it had taken him most of the day to work up the nerve to ask her out. And she'd said no. They'd had fun together at the Memorial Day party. At least he'd thought so. It had seemed like all systems go. What had gone wrong?

Company. What kind of company?

Part of him said to just forget it. That he didn't need the hassle of it. But the biggest part wanted to keep trying. It was a setback, for sure, but not an outright rejection. She'd gone out with Pal Wainright, for heaven's sakes, surely she'd give Tracy a chance. Wouldn't she?

One thing was for sure. This time he would not run and hide.

This time he would stand and fight for what he wanted.

Chapter Ten

On Friday morning Lilly was up and dressed in her own clothes when Frankie entered the kitchen. "I made us coffee," she said proudly.

"Smells good. You look a lot better today, Lilly. I guess a few days on antibiotics did the trick."

"Lord, I couldn't have felt much worse."

Frankie dispensed the morning's medications out of habit and poured herself a cup of coffee. It was strong and bitter, quite possibly the worst coffee she'd ever tasted. How many scoops had Lilly added?

"Does it taste okay?" Lilly asked.

"It's wonderful."

She made toast and they chatted companionably while they ate. When she'd finished, Lilly stood. "I think I'll go on home, Frankie. Thanks for putting me up."

She felt a stab of disappointment. It had been nice having Lilly's company. "Are you sure? You're welcome to stay another day."

"Naw, I got things I need to do at home." She glanced around wistfully. "You sure got a nice place here."

Frankie put the prescriptions and an unopened bottle of ginger ale in a bag. "Here's your medicine. And you might as well take the rest of this pop." On impulse, she threw a loaf of bread and a jar of peanut butter in the bag. "In case you don't feel up to going to the store just yet. Let me get dressed and I'll run you home."

"It's a nice morning, I can walk."

"Don't be silly. I don't mind at all."

"It's not far, Frankie. And the fresh air will do me good."

When Lilly left, the house seemed empty and quiet. Frankie dumped the pot of coffee and started a fresh one, then stripped the guest room bed and threw the sheets in the washer. She fed the kittens and took a shower and watered her plants. Now what? Maybe today she'd start painting the bathroom.

She'd just made out a shopping list for the hardware store when Tracy's truck pulled up in front of her house. Heart galloping, she met him at the door.

"I thought I'd stop by and measure that window again. Is this a good time?"

"It's as good as any. Come in."

He'd gotten some sun since she'd last seen him. His skin looked bronzed against his standard white tee shirt.

"I found a nice double hung window in the shop that I think I can make work for your kitchen." He took out his tape measure and ran it length and widthwise across the window. "It's a little more narrow than what you have, but I can build up the casing."

She smiled. "You're the expert."

He stuffed his tape measure back in his pocket. "Okay. So I guess I'll see you Monday at five thirty."

"Sounds good." Her heart thudded. Did she dare? "Unless…"

He looked at her expectantly. "Unless?"

"Unless you're free for dinner tonight?"

He was clearly surprised, and not unpleasantly. "I could probably manage to be. Where would you like to go?"

"Ahh, anywhere but Sloppy Sue's."

He laughed. "I can definitely do better than that. How about if I pick you up at seven?"

"Perfect."

"Okay. I'll see you then."

She waited until his truck pulled away from the curb, then let out a loud whoop. The article she'd read said it was perfectly fine for a woman to be assertive and make the first move, but she'd never in a million years dreamed she'd have the nerve to do it. But she had. She'd done it! Now to go and find something to wear.

At seven o'clock, with the kittens safely in the guest room, she opened the door to his knock. He'd changed into dark jeans and a white collared shirt. Like Rhoda, he wore clothes well, and though she had chosen her most colorful Lula Roe skirt and top, she felt bland beside him.

"I forgot to ask if you like seafood," he said.

"I love sea food," she told him. Which wasn't entirely true. She wasn't sure whether she liked it or not, since she'd eaten very little of it, aside from the Lenten season fish fries she'd served at school.

He took her to a surf and turf restaurant called Above Board. It was in a nicer section of town, but it wasn't so fancy that it made her feel uncomfortable. Above Board was the perfect first date restaurant.

When they were seated, a waitress brought menus and a basket of cheddar biscuits.

"What do you recommend?" Frankie asked, scanning her menu.

"They're known for their crab cakes. But they also have a very nice Fisherman's Platter. It's got a little bit of everything,"

She closed her menu. "I think I'll get that."

They talked about his current job, an addition he was putting on a dentist's office, until the server arrived with their food. She hadn't eaten since breakfast and the sight of the sea scallops and the shrimp and the oven-broiled flounder nearly made her swoon. "This looks too pretty to eat," she said. She caught his look of amusement and immediately felt foolish. Why did she say such foolish things?

He picked up his fork and went to work on his tilapia.

"So tell me about Frankie Bonetti," he said.

"Hmmm. Actually, I'd rather talk about Tracy." The article had said to engage your date in conversation about themselves. But that wasn't why she'd said it. She really wanted to know about him. She wanted to know everything about him.

"What would you like to know?"

"I can see that you and Rhoda are close. I envy that. Were you always, growing up?"

"We kind of had to be." He took a swallow of water from his glass. "Our father died when I was a junior in high school. Rhoda was in the fifth grade. Mom was a nurse, and she worked twelve-hour days to keep the household going, so Rhodie and I pretty much had to take care of ourselves. Of course I was older, so I tried to fill the role of father for her. And now she acts like a mother to me. Go figure."

"Is your mother gone, too?"

"Yes and no. She's in a nursing home with advanced dementia. She hasn't known me for a long time. Rhoda goes to see her a couple of times a week, but I'm not that faithful about going. It's hard. What about you?"

She told him a little about her parents, and about growing up as an only child. She paused to finish the last of her scallops. "This is such a treat. My husband didn't like seafood, so I rarely ate it."

"How long were you married?"

"Twenty years."

"That's a long time to go without sea food."

"It's a long time to go without a lot of things." Oh, Lord. Now why had she said that? She didn't need a book on relationships to know that trash-talking your dead husband was a huge no-no. She'd promised herself she wasn't going to do that. She quickly steered the conversation back to him.

"I take it you've lived in Port Arthur for a long time."

"All my life. A lot of my classmates took off for bigger and better, but I never really cared about living anyplace bigger than here." He picked up his water glass, twirled it in his hand, and set it back down. "After high school I worked for a construction company. When I'd learned enough to go out on my own, I opened my business in Port Arthur. I bought a house near my old neighborhood. I married the first girl I ever kissed, but not right away. Joanne wanted to finish nursing school first. We got married at twenty-three. We had an ordinary life, but a good life."

"How long has she been gone?"

"Four years." He pulled a wad of money out of his pocket, peeled off a fifty and a ten, and set them on the tray with their bill. "Are you ready to go?"

When they reached her house, they sat out front in his truck. "I really enjoyed myself, Tracy. Thanks so much."

"Thank you for your company."

"I'm sorry if I asked too many questions."

"I asked just as many." He smiled. "That's what a conversation is, isn't it? Give and take. Ebb and flow."

"Yes, I guess it is."

It was a wonderful, stressful moment. She would see him on Monday, but that seemed too long to wait, so she screwed up her nerve and took another chance. "Tracy, would you like to go to church with me on Sunday?"

The question clearly surprised him. "To church?"

"It's just kind of … Going alone … It's lonely. I just thought … Never mind."

"Where would we go?"

"I've been going to St. Bridgette's. It's on Columbus Avenue."

"I'm a member of St. Bridgette's."

Now it was her turn to be surprised. "You are?"

"I haven't gone to mass in years. That's another thing I'm not very faithful about."

She watched him, waiting.

"After Joanne died, I guess I was mad at God, so I stopped going to mass. By the time I got over being angry, I was out of the habit. But sure. I'll go with you on Sunday."

"You will?"

"Is the service still at ten o'clock?"

"Yeah."

"I'll pick you up at a quarter till."

"I'll be ready."

"Frankie?"

"Yes?"

"Can I give you a kiss?"

Her smile widened. "I thought you'd never ask."

He leaned over the console and put his hands on either side of her face. When his lips brushed against hers, she thought she would faint.

The kiss was lovely, lingering.

Oh. My. Goodness.

She could count on one hand the men she'd kissed, and not one of them had ever left her breathless. Until now.

Finally he pulled away. "Goodnight, Frankie."

Somehow she found her voice. "Good night."

He idled at the curb until she was safely in the house, and then slowly drove away.

Part Three
*Those Who Trespass
Against Us*

Chapter Eleven

Frankie counted thirty-seven people at St. Bridgette's on Sunday morning. Every one of them made it a point to speak to Tracy. Somehow, with Tracy by her side, she was no longer invisible. Men smiled at her and women introduced themselves.

People are strange, she thought. Why is it that a middle aged woman needs to have a man beside her in order to be validated? These thoughts occupied her mind as she slid into a pew. Not her usual one in the back, but one right up front, in the third row.

Today, everything seemed different, fresh and new. The baskets of carnations on the altar were a more vivid shade of red. The organ music was sweeter, and the incense that lingered in the air was heady and smoky-sweet. It was as if today she was a little closer to heaven than she'd ever been before.

The prayers seemed to reach higher, and the readings, deeper. That Tracy sat beside her, dressed in navy blue slacks, his hair still damp from the shower, seemed like an incredible gift, and everything, everything was more wonderful because of it. When Father Joe presented the Gospel reading, she eagerly gave him her attention.

"This is the Word of the Lord according to Saint Matthew."

"Thanks be to God."

"In this manner, therefore, pray. 'Our Father in heaven, Hallowed be Your name. Your kingdom come. Your will be done On earth as it is in heaven. Give us this day our daily bread. And forgive us our debts, As we forgive our debtors. And do not lead us into temptation, But deliver us from the evil one. For Yours is the kingdom and the power and the glory forever. Amen.' This is the word of the Lord."

"Glory to You, Lord."

She glanced at her bulletin to see what today's topic would be. *Those Who Trespass Against Us.* Well, she should certainly be able to relate to that. She listened attentively as Father Joe began his homily. He painted a picture of God the Father, seated in the glories of heaven, his will carried out unreservedly. He painted another of how wonderful life would be if God's will were truly done here on earth.

"It's good to pray," he said. "In our prayers, it's important we acknowledge God as the supreme ruler of the universe. Our heavenly father wants us to ask him to meet our needs. He delights to give us our daily bread. But my question for you this morning, dear ones, is this: Do we really want our all-powerful, all-knowing God to forgive us our trespasses as we forgive others theirs? I think not many of us would find ourselves forgiven, if God forgave us the way we forgive others."

His words pierced Frankie's heart. She thought of decades-old hurts and grudges she still held against her parents. Not to mention her husband.

"The eighteenth century poet, Alexander Pope said, To err is human, to forgive is divine. Our Lord Himself said, 'For in the same way you judge others, you will be judged, and with the measure you use, it will be measured to you.' Brothers and sisters, let us pray today for the grace to forgive others as Christ has forgiven us. For His forgiveness was, indeed, divine. Divine, even when his close friend denied knowing his name. Divine, even when he was surrounded by outcasts and murderers and thieves." He paused. "Divine, even as they drove the metal spikes into his hands."

As she knelt after communion, Frankie was too ashamed to pray. She liked to think of herself as a kind, loving, forgiving person. But she realized now that she was none of those things. She had never forgiven her parents, not really. And she certainly hadn't forgiven Alonzo. If she'd heard this homily even a year ago she would have gone home and told him how she felt, no matter how annoyed or angry he might be. She would have overlooked his unkindness and found a way to forgive him. But how did you forgive someone who was dead and buried. God in heaven, her heart cried, I know you were there. You saw it all, everything he did. You heard every word he said. I don't think I can ever forget. Please … show me how to forgive.

After mass, she and Tracy walked out into the brilliant June morning.

"Do you feel like a late breakfast," Tracy asked. "Or maybe an early lunch?"

She wasn't a bit hungry, but she didn't want the date to be over. "Either one would be nice."

He took her to Archie's, an old hotel near the town square that had been converted into a restaurant; a pink stucco, three-story building with rose and white striped awnings. Tucked away behind the restaurant she discovered a large deck with a scattering of tables covered in white linen cloths, jewel colored vases with a single pink rose decorating every one. Flowering trees overhung the dining area and pots of colorful flowers were arranged in haphazard loveliness everywhere she looked. Despite the early hour, strings of white lights twinkled from the trees.

"This looks just like a fairy land," she said in wonder. "Can we eat out here?"

"That was my plan," he said.

They chose a table beneath the branches of a flowering crab tree, its soft, pink petals littering the patio like confetti. There were menus on the table, and Frankie eagerly opened hers. "They have quite a selection here. They even have vegan dishes?"

"This place is about as hipster as Port Arthur gets," Tracy told her. "I remember back when I was a kid this was still a hotel. They called it The Crabtree Inn. Of course, it was pretty run down by then. Believe it or not, Port Arthur used to be an important town, back in the early 1900s. Sitting at the mouth of the Ohio River like it is, it was a prime spot for industry. A lot of important people passed through, and the Crabtree Inn was a showplace. They closed it down in the late seventies and the building sat empty for a lot of years. It's nice to see it open again."

When the server came, Frankie ordered a short stack of ginger oat pancakes and a side order of hash browns. Almost apologetically, Tracy asked for a bacon burger.

"I'm supposed to be limiting my salt," he told her. "But usually, I don't."

The food came quickly and Frankie realized she was hungrier than she'd thought. She dug in with gusto, savoring every buttery, ginger-spiced bite.

"Thanks for going to mass with me today," she said. "Are you glad you went?"

"Sure."

"What did you think of Father Joe's homily?"

"To tell you the truth, it bothered me," he said.

"Me, too."

"Forgiveness is a tough thing sometimes." He picked up his water glass, lightly swirled his water, and set the glass back down. "I wasn't completely honest with you the other day, Frankie. I feel like I should set you straight."

Her stomach squeezed as she wondered what was coming. "All right."

"I told you I didn't have any kids. But I do. I have a son."

She nodded, waiting.

"His name is Dalton."

"Why didn't you tell me you have a son?" she asked gently.

"To be honest, I don't even know if I do anymore."

She watched him intently, wanting to understand.

He took a swallow of water and hesitated, collecting his thoughts. "Joanne and I were twenty-five when he was born, almost the same age he is now. We had all of the usual hopes and dreams that any parents have. I thought someday he'd want to go into business with me. She thought he'd play football for Ohio State. You know how it goes.

"He made us proud. I can't say he didn't. He never gave his mother a minute's worry like some kids do. He got good grades, he was home when he was supposed to be home, even in high school he never got so much as a day's detention. He was finishing his second year of college when Joanne got sick. Or I should say, when she admitted she was sick. She knew,

knew for months and didn't say anything. She said she didn't want to upset Dalton, didn't want to stress him out during his tests. But really, I think she just didn't want to face what she knew was happening. By the time she saw a doctor, it was too late. The cancer had progressed to stage four. The thing is, she was a nurse. She should have known better. "

"How are you guys doing out here?" Frankie jumped. She'd been so intent on what Tracy was saying that she hadn't seen the server approaching.

"Everything's fine," Tracy told him.

"Can I get you anything else?"

"Two cups of coffee, please."

He returned with the coffee and Tracy took a swallow from his cup. Picking up the thread of his conversation, he said, "Losing her hit us hard. Dalton didn't go back to school that next semester. He just couldn't. I gave him a job with the company, but construction wasn't what he wanted to do. His heart just wasn't in it. After his mother died, he stared to change. I was hurting so badly, I guess I didn't see that he was hurting just as much. So he turned to alcohol and pot for the comfort he couldn't find at home."

"Oh, no," she said softly.

"From there it only got worse. He got pulled into harder drugs. It was one long, unending cycle; foolish choices, jail time, promises made, promises broken. Then it would all start again. He was a mess, and I was too much of a mess myself to know what to do for him. One day he stole a hundred dollars from the business. I know it wasn't a great amount of money, but it was the last straw. I lashed out. I threatened to call the cops and have him arrested. He didn't want to go back to jail, so he took off. I stayed angry for a long time. But after a while, I worked through it. I realized he'd taken the money to try and get my attention. And I knew I'd blown it. I wanted my son back, but by then it had been a couple of years and I couldn't find him."

"You haven't seen him since?"

"No."

She reached across the table and covered his hand with hers.

"The thing is, Frankie, I said a terrible thing to him. I'd give anything if I could have that day back, unsay those words, but I can't. I said them. And he believed me."

"What did you say?" she whispered.

Tears gathered in his eyes and he blinked them back. "I told him that from now on he was dead to me. What kind of father says that to his son?"

"I'm sure he knows you didn't mean it," she said softly.

"I'm not sure of that at all. But one thing I am sure of. If there's anyone in the world in need of forgiveness, you're looking at him."

Chapter Twelve

Later that day, Frankie was still thinking about all that had happened. As she sat on her porch, her mind worked on the things Tracy had told her. She didn't know what she should to do with them, if anything. She'd never had children, but she liked to think that in Tracy's situation she would move heaven and earth to find Dalton. But what did she know about the dynamics of a relationship between a father and his son? Her own father had never gone against mother and taken Frankie's side. Not once. But she didn't want to think about that right now.

It was late afternoon when she saw Lilly coming toward her down the sidewalk. She waved. Lilly waved back.

"Girl, where you been all day? I come by here twice before and you weren't here."

"I went to church. Then I went out for lunch. And then for a drive around Lake Arthur."

"With Mister Right?"

"Yes."

"Ooh." She climbed the porch steps and settled herself into a chair. "So go on, tell me all the details."

"There's not a lot to tell. Just a nice, quiet day."

"Hmm." She reached in the pocket of her dress, pulled out four one-dollar bills, and handed them to Frankie. "I got some of that money I owe you. I'll pay some more when I get another load of scrap."

Frankie didn't want the money but she knew there was no point in arguing. She took the bills from Lilly's hand. "It won't leave you short, will it?"

"Nah."

"Okay. Would you like a glass of sweet tea?"

"I wouldn't turn it down."

Frankie went inside and poured them each a glass, then returned to the porch. "Let me ask you something, Lily."

"Okay. Can't promise I'll answer, but you can ask it."

"Have you forgiven your ex-husband for all the things he did?"

"Lord, no. Why would I do that?"

"Something Father Joe said in church this morning has gotten me thinking seriously about Alonzo. I don't think I've forgiven him. I don't think I know how."

"I'll never forgive Harvey for what he done to my children. Not ever."

"But what if that means God won't forgive you?" Frankie asked softly.

"Is that what your preacher said?"

"More or less."

"Well now, I guess I'll have to give that some thought."

They drank their tea without speaking for a while, listening to the quiet sounds of the neighborhood winding down. Finally Frankie asked, "Did you finish all of your medicine?"

"I got four more days' worth left."

"Be sure and take it all. You heard what the nurse said."

"I know."

A robin hopped into the yard in front of them, snagged a small scrap of candy wrapper from the ground, and carried it up into a high branch of the apple tree.

"Now what do you suppose she wants with that?" Frankie asked.

"Padding for her nest," Lilly replied. "It ain't the fanciest thing, but sometimes you just got to be thankful for what the Good Lord gives you. That I do know for a fact."

•

The next morning Frankie was up early. She sat at her table, drinking her first cup of coffee of the day and making a list. Last night she'd spent some time researching plants for her cottage garden. She'd decided on a small patch of herbs and some colorful wildflowers. She wanted to pick up some groceries today. She'd pick up seed packets at the grocery store, she decided. It would be slower than buying established plants, but much cheaper. She still had a list as long as her arm of home improvements to pay for.

Basil. Chives. Oregano. Mixed flowers. She chewed the end of her pen, thought for a moment, and then continued her list. Lasagna noodles. Ricotta cheese. Garlic bread.

Tracy would be coming to install the new window today and she planned to surprise him with dinner.

She folded her list and put it in her purse. She'd also bookmarked a You Tube video that looked interesting, a teaching on forgiveness. But she'd watch that later. She had a lot to do, and she wanted to get at the garden before the Southern Ohio day grew too humid.

The supermarket was busy for a Monday morning. After spending more time looking at garden goodies than she'd planned to, she hurried home and changed into her old jeans. The sunshine was glorious and she spent the afternoon listening to the chatter of birds and the weekday sounds of the neighborhood as she worked up the soil and planted her seeds.

After giving them a good soaking, she eagerly put together the small, stained glass birdbath she'd bought in the supermarket garden section. It was more money than she should have spent, but as the sun glinted off the reds, golds and greens, she pictured how lovely it would be surrounded by sun-drenched coreopsis and sky blue bachelor's buttons and knew it was worth every penny she'd spent.

Back inside, she put together a pan of lasagna and set it in the fridge. She'd pop it into the oven just before Tracy got there. With nothing left to do, she ran a tub of water for a bath and selected a book from her cabinet.

When Tracy arrived that evening, she met him at the door, dressed in her black capris and a white peasant top.

"Hello, pretty lady" he said, smiling.

"Hello, yourself."

He gave her a quick kiss and went to work unloading the building materials from his truck.

They chatted while he worked, Frankie holding the tools and handing them to him as he asked for them.

"You make a good contractor," he said. "Maybe I'll hire you on as an apprentice."

"Ahh, I'll keep that in mind if my new job doesn't work out."

He sniffed the air. "What is that amazing smell?"

"Dinner."

"Really?"

"Payback is sweet. You've bought me a brunch and a dinner so far, and now it's my turn to treat you."

He complimented her lasagna over and over again, taking second helpings of everything. "I could get used to this lasagna pretty easy," he said.

She smiled. She could get used to making it for him just as easily. She liked the way he looked sitting at her table, liked the easy give and take of their conversation. And though she wanted to keep it light and upbeat, she felt the need to say what was in her heart.

"Tracy, I've been thinking about the thing we talked about on Sunday."

"Which thing is that?"

"About Dalton. Maybe you could hire a private detective to look for him. Maybe they could find him for you."

His expression clouded. "And then what, Frankie? Drag him back home?"

"I don't know, I just thought ..."

"I've thought of that, too. More than once. But I've decided I don't want to force him. I don't want to try and find him if he doesn't want to be found. He knows where I am. I keep hoping that someday, when he's ready, he'll come to me."

She would have liked to explore a few different options with him, but she knew by the finality of his tone that the discussion was over.

They went over her list of projects and decided that the laundry room ceiling would be next. "That might have to wait until I can free up a bigger block of time. But I'll bring a new faucet for your tub tomorrow."

She grinned. "And they say you have to wait weeks to get a

good contractor."

"Not when you cook like this, babe."

The endearment sent a warm glow washing over her heart.

After he left, she picked up her book, then set it back down. She felt too restless to read. She went to her desktop, sat down, and pulled up the video she'd bookmarked.

The speaker was an attractive woman of about her age, and Frankie was immediately drawn to the lively and energetic presentation. She found herself nodding as the woman talked about old hurts and memories.

"The secret to forgiveness is to not to block them out, or deny their existence," she said. "The secret is to let them come. Let the memories come, and allow yourself feel what you feel. And then give those feelings; that hurt, that anger, over to God and let him heal you. He loves you, and he wants to make you whole again."

She went to bed pondering the things the woman said. She would give it a try. But not tonight. Tonight she would not think about Alonzo. Not when she would so much rather think about Tracy.

•

She was incredible.

At midnight Tracy sat on his deck, unable to sleep. His mind and heart were filled with Frankie, and the amazing treasure he'd found in her. She was beautiful, sweet, and generous. And she sure made a mean lasagna.

His thoughts turned inward. She probably thought he was a failure as a father. He'd seen it in her eyes when she'd suggested hiring a private detective to find Dalton and he'd shut the conversation down. She thought he should pursue his son.

He'd thought of that, too. But somehow, he couldn't.

It wasn't that he couldn't forgive Dalton. He'd forgiven him months ago. And it wasn't that he wouldn't love to find him and bring him home where he belonged. Home, warm and safe beneath Tracy's roof, like when he was small.

What it was, was fear. Fear that he might find Dalton, and

find himself unforgiven. Rejected by the person he loved the most. His child. His and Joanne's. The pain of that would be more than his battered heart could bear.

Chapter Thirteen

In the middle of the week Frankie took the kittens to be neutered. She'd made the appointment two weeks before, but with one thing and another, she hadn't gotten around to buying a cat carrier. In the back seat, they howled from the Rubbermaid tote she'd put them in, peering mournfully at her through the cloudy plastic. She was glad it was only a ten minute drive to the vet's office. The howling was setting her teeth on edge.

Inside, the office was sleek and bright, more upscale than many human doctors' offices Frankie had been to. She was embarrassed by the tote, and vowed to go out and get a proper cat carrier that very day. She still needed paint for her bedroom. Maybe she would stop at Walmart after dropping off the cats and kill two birds with one stone.

She gave her name at the front desk, and was given a stack of forms to fill out. Finding an empty seat in the waiting area, she dug her reading glasses out of her purse and scanned the form on top of the stack. She would have to leave some of the spaces blank, she realized. She had no idea how old the cats were, or what their family history was.

A small buff-colored poodle eyed the tote on the floor beside her, perking up as an orange paw reached out through the air hole she'd cut into the top. Whining softly, the dog inched closer and lapped at the paw with his tongue. The paw darted back inside.

"Don't mind Baxter, he loves cats," his owner, an elderly woman, said.

"Aren't you a nice boy," Frankie crooned, petting the dog's

fuzzy head. His soft brown eyes looked up into hers and she fell in love. Maybe she would think about getting a dog of her own. She'd always liked them, though she'd never owned one. They couldn't be that much different than cats, could they?

After a lengthy wait, a vet tech came to collect Nutmeg and Pepper. The cats looked at her through the cloudy plastic as the girl carried them away, making Frankie want to cry. With a pang and a promise to pick them up the next morning, she left the office.

In Walmart, she selected a carrier large enough for two full-grown cats, threw a bag of food and two boxes of litter into her cart, and headed for the store's home improvement section. After carefully considering all the paint choices, she settled on a white-tinted-rose for the bedroom and bought a second gallon for the guest room.

She wouldn't be seeing Tracy until Friday, so she may as well jump into the painting with both feet. She'd just gotten through the check-out line when she heard her name. Glancing up, she saw Rhoda and Allie walking toward her.

"Hey, stranger!"

"Hi Rhoda. Hello, Allie."

"What brings you out to Wally World today?"

"I had to get a cat carrier, and I thought it might be a good day to start painting the bedroom."

Rhoda inspected the paint can. "That's a nice color."

"I hope it will look as nice on the walls as it does on this chip. Have you got time for lunch? I was just thinking about getting a calzone."

"I wish I did. I have an open house I've got to get back to. But someone lost her cell phone. Again. And for some reason she thinks she has to have a new one right this minute."

"I'm going to go look, Mom," Allie said. "I know just what I want."

"You're getting another Straight Talk phone."

"Mom!"

"We talked about this. I'm not buying you an expensive phone until I can trust you not to lose them. Be glad you're getting anything at all. I'll be there in a minute. Don't go wandering off."

Allie rolled her eyes. "Mom, I'm fourteen, not four!"
"I know." She turned to Frankie almost apologetically. "Guy says I smother her, but I can't help it. You hear about things happening, even in a town the size of Port Arthur."

"You're just doing your job."

"Tell them that. So anyway, how's the house coming along? Tracy said he fixed that window."

"It's getting there, little by little."

"I'm glad I ran into you today. I was actually going to call you later."

"You were?"

"I was going to ask if you and Tracy wanted to come over on Saturday night. I thought we could get a pizza, maybe play some cards."

"That sounds like fun."

"Good. I'll have you ask him, then. He gets annoyed when he thinks I'm bugging him, though I really haven't seen much of him since the Memorial Day party."

"He's been busy with work."

"I heard you took him to church."

Frankie was taken aback. Was there anything Rhoda didn't know?

"Sorry, I don't mean to be nosy, it's just … I'm so happy the two of you have hit it off. I worry about him."

Frankie smiled. "That's another of your jobs, isn't it?"

"Well, yes, it is. But truthfully I wouldn't mind handing that one off to you." She laughed. "I've got my hands full with Guy and Allie. I'd better run, before she sets her mind on a smart phone. I'll see you Saturday. Around seven-ish?"

"We'll be there," she said, but Rhoda was already making her way toward the electronics department.

She'd intended to go to Luigi's and get carryout for lunch, but something made her drive past the church. On impulse, she pulled into the parking lot and walked up to the back door. Finding it unlocked, she went inside and quietly slipped into a pew. Here it was, already Wednesday, and she hadn't made a bit of progress toward forgiving anyone.

God, I really want to do this, she prayed. *I really want to let go of my grudges and let you heal me.*

With her head bowed, she knelt in silence, waiting for the memories to come, like the woman said. She tried to block out the noise of the traffic in the street outside, and the creaks and groans of the hundred-year-old building.

Let them come, she told herself.

She tried to quiet her thoughts, to relax and let Alonzo's memory come naturally into focus. But when a memory finally came, it was not her husband that showed up. It was her mother.

She must have been about five or six years old. She and her mother had stopped at the shopping plaza after school. Her mother had needed a birthday gift and a roll of wrapping paper, so they'd gone to Woolworth's. Frankie lingered by a big cage full of parakeets, watching with enchantment as they shrieked to her, bobbing their green and yellow heads.

Her mother hadn't noticed she'd lagged behind, and when Frankie looked up, she was alone. She remembered the terror of that moment as if it was yesterday. It was probably only a matter of minutes, but to her it had seemed an eternity.

"This is painful," she whispered.

She went rushing through the store, crying, calling for her mother. A sweet-faced old woman knelt beside her. "What's wrong, baby? Have you lost your mommy?"

Just then Frankie looked up to see her mother marching toward her. She grabbed Frankie by the arm and shook her roughly.

"I thought I told you to stay with me!"

"I'm sorry, mama. I was looking at the birds."

Her mother's displeasure rolled over her like tidal wave. "You've always got an excuse, haven't you? God doesn't like little girls who disobey, haven't I told you that? Haven't I?" She shook her again. "I hope you got a good look at your birds today, Francesca, because I'll never bring you to the plaza again. Now march!"

She sat in the pew, unable to stop her tears from rolling down her cheeks as she let herself feel the pain of that long-suppressed memory. And there were others.

The open house at her elementary school, and how mother had stopped to talk with lovely Mrs. Apsley, her second grade teacher. Mrs. Apsley had told mother what a good little helper Frankie was.

"I only wish she would apply herself to her school work as much as she does to clapping erasers," Mother had grumbled. "You'd never know both of her parents are educators with the poor grade cards that child brings home."

Mrs. Apsley had smiled at Frankie, but even that wasn't enough to ease the pain of mother's words.

What had the woman in the video said? Give it to God.

How did you go about doing that, exactly?

God, I was just a little girl. I tried so hard to please her. She never had any patience with me. I'm finding it very hard to forgive my mother for being so hateful all the time. For making me feel unloved. So I'm going to do what the woman in the video said. I'm going to give it to you. So here it is…

She heard a creak and looked up as Father Joe stepped softly into the pew. He regarded her with his wise, kind eyes. "What's bothering you, child?"

"I was just… praying about some things." She wiped at her tears with the backs of her hands. "I'm trying to forgive my mother," she said simply. "I don't think she ever loved me."

"You don't think so?"

She shook her head. "I'm really not sure if anyone ever has."

"I can't speak for your mother, but I can promise you, your heavenly Father has loved you from the moment you were conceived in your mother's womb."

Frankie gave him a small smile. "I guess I forget that sometimes."

"Love is a complicated thing, whether it's between husbands and wives, parent and children, or friends. For every person that tells me someone didn't love them, I have two who tell me they wished they'd done a better job of it. Sometimes people love, and have trouble showing that they do."

She nodded.

"And sometimes we have to look beyond our disappointments in other people and ask God to help us see the times he has loved us through others."

"I'll try to do that, Father."

He patted her arm. "You're welcome to stay as long as you need to."

As he disappeared through a door behind the altar, she returned again to those long-ago memories. She thought of Mrs. Apsley's smile, and of the kind old woman in Woolworth's and the soft way she'd spoken to her. Had it been God's face, looking out at her through theirs?

When her mother had finally appeared, the old woman had asked, "Is this your little girl?"

Her mother had said something Frankie could not remember. But just before that, before she unleashed her wrath, had there been a look of relief on her mother's face, if only for a moment? Had her mother been as scared as she was, and had her fear come crashing out in the form of anger? Or did Frankie just want to think it was so?

She looked at the statue in front of her, Jesus with a small lamb cradled in his arms.

"Help me," she whispered.

The Jesus statue seemed to gaze back at her, loving and benevolent. She took a deep shuddering breath and made herself say the words.

"I forgive you, Mama."

Her mother's voice seemed to echo down through time. *Now say it like you mean it!*

"I. Forgive. You."

Leaving the church, she didn't know if she really meant it or not. But she knew she wanted to. Maybe in time, she would be able to feel some love and forgiveness for her mother. Or maybe it wasn't important to feel it. Maybe a person just had to believe it. In any case, she felt lighter for having shed the memory.

Chapter Fourteen

On Saturday night she and Tracy arrived at Rhoda and Guy's house at seven o'clock. After ushering them inside, Guy offered them each a beer. "Have a seat. Rhoda's upstairs, let me run up and tell her you're here."

As Frankie took her place on the sofa, a small dog approached her warily, his hackles raised.

"Oh, how cute are you?"

"That's Sassy," Tracy told her. "I wouldn't encourage him, if I were you."

"But he's adorable. Come here, Sassy." She held out her hand for him to sniff. He prowled closer, his nose quivering as he tested the air. She must have passed inspection, because he jumped into her lap.

"That's pretty amazing. That dog hates everyone. Especially me."

"I'm sure he doesn't hate you," she said, patting the dog's head.

"Yes he does. Look at this." He extended his hand. "Come here, Sassy."

The dog barred his tiny teeth and growled.

"Oh my goodness, you naughty little boy. Tell me, what do have against Tracy?"

"When he was just a pup I accidentally stepped on his foot. He's never forgotten it. I think he could use one of Father Joe's sermons on forgiveness."

Laughing, she scratched the dog's ears and he snuggled against her. "I've been thinking about getting a dog."

"Are your cats going to be all right with that?"

"They'd probably get used to it. I don't think they'd feel threatened if I were to get a small dog like Sassy. He's not much bigger than they are, are you Sassy? " The dog licked her hand.

"Hey, guys," Rhoda said, walking into the room. "Sorry to keep you waiting."

"Rhodie, Frankie wants your dog."

"Really?" Guy grinned. "Quick, go and get his doggie bones and his pee-pee pads before she changes her mind."

"He doesn't mean that," Rhoda said. "He loves that dog more than any of us do. Are you ready to play cards?"

Frankie reluctantly set the wiggling dog on the floor and followed Rhoda to the dining room, where she'd set out a cheese and cracker plate, along with a tray of fresh veggies. Three decks of cards sat in the middle of the table. "I didn't know what everybody would want to play. This is what I have for cards, or there's a cupboard full of board games."

Frankie examined her choices. "I've never played Phase Ten."

"It's a lot of fun," Rhoda told her.

"Ahh, it's a lot of fun until Rhoda starts losing," Guy corrected.

Rhoda shot him an annoyed glance and they took their places at the table, with Sassy camped out at Frankie's feet.

"I'll put him in the kitchen," Guy said, "Come here, Sassy boy."

"He's fine," Frankie protested.

"Okay, but don't make any sudden moves. He bites when he gets nervous."

Tracy explained the rules of the game as Rhoda dealt the cards.

"It sounds kind of complicated," Frankie worried.

"You'll get the hang of it."

They weren't very far into the game before Frankie discovered the group was as competitive in cards as they were in water volleyball. They played boisterously, slapping down cards, protesting loudly when things didn't go the way they wanted, celebrating even more loudly when they did.

When Tracy and Rhoda started swapping embarrassing

family stories, Frankie thought she'd die laughing.

The first game ended with Tracy the winner just as the doorbell rang.

"That must be the pizza." Guy left the room. He talked with the delivery person for a moment and then returned to the dining room carrying two large pizza boxes.

"One would probably have been enough," Tracy said.

As Rhoda set out plates, napkins, and bottles of pop, Allie bounded down the stairs.

"Thanks for telling me the pizza was here."

"Allie, the pizza's here," Tracy hollered.

She shoved him, then grabbed two slices from the box and headed back to her room.

"It's probably a good thing we got two after all," Rhoda said. "I swear that girl's having some sort of a growth spurt this summer. For the last few weeks she's been eating us out of house and home."

"I wouldn't exactly say that," Guy said.

"What exactly would you say, then? Last week an entire box of granola bars and a bottle of Pepsi disappeared in one day. This week it was an entire jar of peanut butter."

"If you ask me a few pounds wouldn't hurt her in the least," Tracy said.

Frankie excused herself to use the bathroom. Outside her bedroom door, she overheard Allie talking on her cell phone. "I think you should give him a chance... Because he's a really good guy... You shouldn't feel that way, though. No, I won't ... I won't say anything to him, I promise."

She smiled. She loved teenaged girls with all of their secrets and mystery. Many times at St. Sebastian's the older girls had come to her for advice about boys, which she found amusing, considering she'd barely dated in the years before she married Alonzo. Those twelve-year-old girls probably had more experience with relationships than she did.

After another round of cards, which Guy won, they put the cards away and talked until well after midnight. Despite her best efforts, Frankie couldn't stop yawning.

"We should take off," Tracy said. "We've got church in the morning."

Rhoda caught Frankie's eye and smiled.

Back at her·house, they sat in his truck. "Thanks for putting up with us again," Tracy said. "I know we can be a little overwhelming sometimes."

"Are you kidding? I love you guys."

He took her face in his hands and kissed her, a long, slow, sweet kiss. "We love you too, Frankie Bonetti."

•

The next weekend they played cards with Rhoda and Guy again, and the weekend after that they went to the movies.

Frankie had never double dated before. Growing up under her father's watchful eye she'd never done much of anything. She felt as though at fifty she'd finally been given the adolescence she'd never had. On the Fourth of July she and Tracy sat on blankets beside the lake, holding hands and murmuring quietly together and she didn't know how life could be any sweeter.

July melted into a magical month of candlelit dinners, after-church brunches, and walks around the lake. Each date ended with a kiss, and Frankie knew he didn't expect anything more. Tracy Johanson was a gentleman, and she was swept away in the wonder of being his lady. It was the most enchanting summer of her life and she never wanted it to end.

When she wasn't with Tracy, she filled her time with working on the house, pulling weeds in her garden, and sporadic, delightful visits on the front porch with Lilly. Since the day at the vet's office, she had become obsessed with dogs. She found websites for all of the local pounds and dog rescues. She poured over them, falling in love with each furry face she saw.

She researched different breeds and their temperaments, trying to decide what kind of dog would be a good match for her and the cats. The house definitely needed a dog, she decided. A small one, like Sassy, but one that was much less territorial.

She didn't have a big enough yard for a large dog to play in, and besides, she'd seen women being walked by their dogs, dragged along in the wake of German shepherds, boxers and chow chows. She didn't have the physical strength for that, but what to get? A corgi? A Jack Russel? A toy poodle? But as she struggled to decide, fate made the choice for her.

She'd just come out of the Home Depot, and was loading the area rug she'd bought for the guest room into the trunk, when a van pulled slowly into the parking lot. She wouldn't have noticed it at all, if not for its loud exhaust.

She glanced up just as the door slid open and man roughly pushed a dog out. The door slid shut with a bang and the van raced away, backfiring. She stared after it in stunned silence, then back at the dog. It cowered in the parking lot, trembling with fear.

She approached it slowly, speaking softly. "It's okay, girl. It's okay."

The dog gazed at her hopefully, and she could see that it was indeed a female, a medium-sized terrier of some sort, mostly white, with a horseshoe-shaped ring around its left eye.

"What did they do to you, girlie?" she asked. "Oh, you poor girlie girl." The dog's stubby tail quivered slightly. She squatted down and stretched forth her hand.

The dog approached cautiously. When she'd sniffed Frankie's hand, she allowed herself to be petted. Up close, Frankie could see that the dog was older, and very skinny. She could almost see her ribs beneath her filthy coat.

"Let's go and get you something to eat, then we'll figure out what to do next."

The dog waited patiently in the car while Frankie ran back in the store and bought dog food, a tie out chain, a collar, and two dishes. She had no idea what the dog might like, so she added a box of dog biscuits and a rawhide chew to her cart as well.

Back home, she tied the dog to her back deck, filled one of the dishes with water, and the other with food, and carried them outside while the kittens watched warily from the window, their tails whipping.

The dog ate sparingly but she drank the entire bowl of water. "Oh, you poor thirsty girl," Frankie murmured. "They didn't take very good care of you, did they, sugar?"

The dog gazed intently into her face and wagged her stubby tail.

"Is that your name, huh? Is your name Sugar? Well, you'll fit right in here then, won't you?"

The dog barked.

She bathed Sugar with her garden hose, dried her with a bath towel, and took her inside. The kittens were overjoyed with their new playmate, but Sugar didn't seem very interested in them at all. She curled up on the blanket Frankie laid out for her in the kitchen and fell asleep.

The kittens soon grew tired of playing with the buckle on Sugar's collar and curled up beside her for a nap. Frankie watched them, her heart overflowing with joy. Sugar was the perfect dog for her and the kittens. Her life had never seemed more full.

"Thank you, God," she whispered. "Thank you for all of these beautiful souls you've given me to love."

July brought other changes as well, changes from within. As if that quiet afternoon in the church had opened the floodgates of her heart, memories of her past surfaced almost daily. Some of them were of Alonzo, and some of her parents. Some were of people she'd forgotten existed. As each one came, she embraced it and set it free. And in the process she was freed herself.

Chapter Fifteen

By the first day of August, Tracy had finished nearly every project on Frankie's list. The broken staircase railing was the last task, and he'd promised to get started on it that day. When he arrived, she met him on the porch. She was nervous, and not sure exactly why. She didn't need a man's permission for anything anymore; she made her own decisions now. But somehow, she wanted Tracy's stamp of approval on everything she did.

"Hey, lady," he said, scooping her up for a hug and kiss.

"I have something to tell you," she blurted.

"Okay."

"I got a dog."

"You did? When?"

"Yesterday. It was crazy. I was in the parking lot of the Home Depot and this van pulled in and well, they just dumped her out. I didn't know what to do."

"So you brought her home."

"Yes. I know you probably think I'm crazy and impulsive."

She waited for a sign, a frown or a roll of his eyes that would show his disapproval. But he didn't do either of those things.

He smiled, cupped her face in his hands, and kissed her again.

"What I think is that you've got a very big heart." He grinned. "I also think you're going to need a bigger house if you keep collecting animals like this."

She smiled. "Come in and meet her."

Inside, she called the dog. The kittens came running and rubbed around Tracy's ankles. Sugar approached cautiously.

"Oh, she's a pit bull?"

"She is?"

"Sure looks like one to me." He squatted. "Come here, girl."

Sugar glanced at Frankie, her cloudy eyes full of questions.

"It's all right," she assured her.

The dog slunk over to Tracy and sniffed him. He scratched her ears and she lay down and offered him her belly. "She seems pretty calm."

"She doesn't have a mean bone in her body. And she gets along really well with Nutmeg and Pepper."

"Pit bulls have a bad reputation, but that doesn't mean they're all bad dogs. I was just surprised you'd take one in. I thought you wanted a small dog."

"I thought I did, too. Until I met Sugar."

Tracy got out his tools and went to work. He removed the railing and the broken spindles, then went about screwing the new ones into place. Frankie sat on the top step while the cats played with the hinges on Tracy's tool box. Afraid of the roar of the power tools, Sugar retreated to her blanket in the kitchen.

"Tell me again what this thing is you have to go to tomorrow," Tracy said.

"It's an orientation. I'll probably be filling out paperwork and watching the same old videos about sanitation, food safety, and safe lifting that I've watched for thirty years." She sighed. "I can't believe I'm starting a new job in less than three weeks."

"Are you excited?"

"I'm excited, yes. I'm also kind of nervous. I hope I'll do all right."

"I'm sure you'll do great, Frankie. The last guy thought enough of your work to recommend you for the job, and the new guy hired you after your first interview. That's got to mean something, doesn't it?"

She smiled. "I guess so."

He leaned over and lightly kissed her lips. "I know so."

●

His confidence in her gave her a much needed shot of courage. The next morning she got up early, took extra care with her hair and makeup, and set out for Holy Child Academy. The south side of Port Arthur was the city's oldest neighborhood.

Driving past the abandoned buildings with their broken windows and tattered awnings, she could still see vestiges of the neighborhood's earlier charm in its architecture and the old gas street lamps that lined the streets.

Like so many small cities across Ohio, poverty had crept in with the loss of industry, and crime skyrocketed with the shocking advent of pill mills and prescription drug abuse. In Port Arthur, all of the ugliness seemed to have settled in this bleak little neighborhood.

A block from the school, she stopped at a red light. In front of a pawn shop, she noticed a rusty red wagon that looked a lot like Lilly's. She craned her neck to see if there was any sign of her friend. She knew Lilly must live somewhere nearby. She always walked from this direction. As the light changed, Frankie drove slowly past the houses along Cleveland Avenue. She took a good look at the sagging porches, the broken sidewalks, the air of hopelessness that hung in the air like thick, gray fog.

She tried to imagine which one of the houses, if any, might belong to her friend. She hated that Lilly had to live in a neighborhood like this. Lilly, who was so full of life and fun.

Distracted, she didn't realize she'd driven past Toledo Avenue until several blocks later. She made a right-hand turn and circled back, as nervous as if it were her first day of kindergarten. She pulled into the parking lot, drew a calming breath, and got out of the car.

And then, one hundred and ninety-seven days after she'd walked out the back door of St. Sebastian's Catholic School for the last time, she walked through the front door of Holy Child Academy.

The walls were bright white and smelled of fresh paint, with the school's emblem proudly displayed above the front door. The green and white checkered tiles gleamed beneath her feet, freshly polished. Her footsteps echoed as she walked to the cafeteria, where she was told the orientation would be held.

Holy Child was much larger than St. Sebastian's had been, with twelve classrooms, a library and computer lab, a cafeteria, a gym and a chapel. St. Sebastian's School had occupied the upper floor of St. Sebastian's church. It had only five classrooms, with kindergarten occupying the smallest one, and the larger ones doubled up; first and second, third and fourth, fifth and sixth, and seventh and eighth grades each sharing a classroom. The parish hall adjacent to the school had served as cafeteria, gym and auditorium. She thought of their motto, Small but Mighty, and felt a stab of homesickness as she walked through Holy Child's large, echoing hallways.

In the cafeteria, she saw that several people were already seated around a table. Tony Argenteri smiled at her warmly as she walked in.

"Here she is now. Good to see you again, Frankie."

She made an apology for being late and slid into the nearest empty seat.

"Okay, let's start with introductions. As you all know, I'm Tony. I'm the principal here, the head honcho, as they say. But I like to think of our staff as family. So if there's ever anything I can do for any of you, please don't hesitate to let me know. This lady to my right is Chelsea Regal, my new assistant principal."

Chelsea Regal could have been twenty-five, thirty-five, or anywhere in between. The older Frankie got, the harder it was for her to tell how old people were.

Chelsea was a pretty woman with perfectly white teeth and long, chestnut-colored hair streaked with blonde highlights. "I'll be in charge of public relations and fundraising, disciplining the students when necessary, and I'll also be your immediate supervisor," she said. "Do what's expected of you and we won't have any problems. Essentially, I expect the staff to be here on the days they're supposed to be, and to be here on time." Her glance skimmed over Frankie, and Frankie's face burned with embarrassment.

Really? She couldn't have been more than five minutes late, at most.

Realizing it was her turn to speak, she cleared her throat.

"Hi, everyone. I'm Frankie Bonetti. I'll be overseeing the cafeteria."

Next up was Katie Ferro, a new fifth grade teacher who looked young enough to be a student herself, and after Katie, there was Lainey, a teacher aide who looked even younger. Finally Joe introduced the only young man at the table.

"Frankie, this is Scat, your new right hand man. He'll be helping you out in the kitchen three mornings a week."
She smiled. "Hello, Scat."

He nodded and smiled back. He was young, maybe twenty years old, a dark, thin boy who bordered on being gaunt. Frankie thought he looked like he needed a steak dinner and a week-long nap.

They filled out the necessary paperwork, then, as she'd suspected, sat through what seemed like a hundred health and safety videos. Tony had arranged to have their lunch brought in—calzones and salads from a nearby pizzeria. After lunch, they went over the school handbook and policies, and then Tony told Lainey and Scat they were free to leave. Frankie and Katie, as fulltime employees, stayed to select and sign up for their benefits packages.

With orientation over, Frankie went to check out her office in the back of the cafeteria. It was a small, no-frills room with a desk, a laptop, and a file cabinet. She was just entering her new password into her school email account when Chelsea breezed in and dumped a stack of paperwork on her desk.

"I brought you some of the spreadsheets I'd like you to use to plan each month's meals. You'll also be doing all of the food and supply ordering, so the catalogues are there too. Orders have to go out the last Thursday of each month. All of your menus and orders will have to be approved by me, so I'd like them a week ahead, if possible."

"All right, that's no problem," Frankie said.

"Good." She breezed from the room without so much as a 'welcome to the team.' Frankie shut down the laptop. She leafed through the stack of papers Chelsea brought. She'd never used spreadsheets before, and they looked confusing. At St. Sebastian's she'd scribbled her menus on notebook paper. And she'd never had to answer to anyone for the meals she planned and served. Once again she felt a pang of homesickness. This was going to be a whole different ball game. Now that she'd made the team, she hoped she wouldn't strike out.

She'd just arrived home and fed the animals when her cell phone rang. Tracy. She smiled. He'd told her he would be working late and wouldn't be free for dinner, but that he'd call to see how her orientation went.

"Hey, how'd it go today?" he asked.

"Okay."

"Just okay?"

"It seems like a good school. Most of the people I met today seem really nice."

"But...?"

"To be honest, I feel a little intimidated by my supervisor. I don't think she likes me."

"Why do you say that?"

Unlike Alonzo, who would have dismissed her fears and accused her of being paranoid, Tracy listened and sympathized as she told him about Chelsea's high-and-mighty attitude.

"She does sound a little overbearing. Do you need me to go down there?"

She heard the smile in his voice, and it made her smile, too. "I don't think that will be necessary at this point, but I'll let you know."

After the phone call, she changed out of her good clothes and went outside to water her flowers. She put Sugar on her chain so she could lie in the sunshine, then filled her watering can and gave the herbs a good soaking. The garden had really taken off. She'd been using the chives in her salads for a couple of weeks now, and soon her oregano would be ready to harvest.

"Girl, look at you with them flowers all in bloom! Ain't you a regular Misses Green Thumbs!" She glanced up to see Lilly heading toward her. "What'd you do now, get you a pit bull?" She told Lilly the story of the van and how they'd dumped Sugar out in the Home Depot parking lot. "I was going to take her to the pound, but after I got her home, well, she seemed so happy and content here, I just couldn't bring myself to do it."

"You know what you are? You're a regular St. Frankie of Assisi."

"Ha ha."

"The flowers look good."

"They do, don't they? I just love all of the colors together. If you hadn't suggested the cottage garden, I would never have thought of putting one in."

Lilly reached down and stroked Sugar's head. "I had me one of these once. Best dog I ever owned. I used to leave him in the yard when the kids was outside playing. I never had to worry about no one bothering them, and that's a fact."

"She doesn't seem to have a lot of energy, but she's just starved for attention. I hope she won't be lonely when I start work."

"When do you start?"

"The first day of school is the eighteenth, but I'll have to start going in next week. I have to get my meals planned and my shopping lists approved. I want them to be perfect."

"Are them kids that fussy over there?"

"It's not the kids I'm worried about. I'm hoping to make a good impression on my supervisor." She told Lilly about the orientation, and about Chelsea Regal's coolness toward her. "I guess I'm having a hard time starting over."

"Anybody would, honey."

"It's just… I was at St. Sebastian's for so many years I felt like I was a part of the building, like I was as much a fixture as the stained-glass windows, or the old slate blackboards. Here, I don't know where I stand. I just hope I'll fit in."

"Frankie, if anybody down there can't get along with you, then they can't get along with nobody."

"Thanks. Hey, I think I almost saw you today."

Lilly gave Sugar another pat on the head and stood up. "What do you mean?"

"I think I saw your red wagon in front of a shop on the corner of Cleveland Avenue and Pine Streets. Don't you live over there somewhere?"

"Sort of."

"Maybe someday I can stop in and visit you on my lunch break."

"I'm not usually around much during the day," she said quickly.

"I could pick you up after school then. We could go out for supper."

"I don't like to go out to eat so much."

"Oh. Okay then. It was just a thought."

"You enjoy the rest of the day, now. I'll see you later."

As she turned and walked away, Frankie realized she'd embarrassed her friend. Lilly obviously didn't want Frankie to see her house and she kicked herself for having said anything.

Part Four

Count it all Joy

Chapter Sixteen

Ever since Tracy started accompanying her to mass, Frankie felt comfortable at St. Bridgette's. She even had a couple of women she chatted with regularly before mass each week. One of them was Mary-Margarete Malloy, a woman Tracy had gone to school with.

"Just watch what you say to her," he'd cautioned.

"Why do you say that?"

"This town's grapevine has roots that spread clear across the county. And a lot of its fertilizing gets done right here at St. Bridgette's. I'm sure Mary's dying to know what's going on with us."

I'm dying to know what's going on with us, Frankie thought, but stopped herself from saying. After that, she was friendly, but not overly forthcoming with information about herself. No matter how persistent Mary-Margaret was in her questioning.

On the first Sunday in August Frankie overslept and the organ was already playing when she and Tracy arrived at mass. She gave Mary-Margaret a quick wave as she slid into her pew.

She and Tracy had sat on her porch last night, talking late into the night. She'd told him stories about her job at St. Sebastian's and confessed her fears about starting over again at Holy Child. He'd talked about Joanne and about Dalton, confessing fears of his own. They'd covered miles of territory, and yet she was no closer to knowing whether the feelings she had for him were mutual. That question had kept her tossing and turning in her bed until the early hours of morning. It occupied her mind as Mary Margaret walked up to the ambo and she realized she'd heard the first reading without hearing it at all.

"Our second reading is from the book of James," Mary-Margaret said. "My brethren, count it all joy when you fall into various trials, knowing that the testing of your faith produces patience. But let patience have its perfect work, that you may be perfect and complete, lacking nothing. If any of you lacks wisdom, let him ask of God, who gives to all liberally and without reproach, and it will be given to him. But let him ask in faith, with no doubting, for he who doubts is like a wave of the sea driven and tossed by the wind. For let not that man suppose that he will receive anything from the Lord; he is a double-minded man, unstable in all his ways. This is the word of the Lord."

"Thanks be to God."

After giving the Gospel reading, Father Joe began his homily. "Trials are a part of life," he said. "You can't be human and not have them. And as humans, we sometimes find it difficult to understand what the apostle James means when he says to 'count it all joy.' But when looked at from God's perspective, knowing that He uses all of the various troubles and trials of life to strengthen our faith, we can appreciate them more fully, if not joyfully. We can bear them more patiently, knowing that God is with us in the midst of them, just as he was with the great men and women of the faith."

He went on to cite Job's sufferings, Daniel in the lion's den, and the Apostle Paul's imprisonment for his faith. "Each of those saints needed wisdom to survive their trials, as each of us do, ours. So let us ask of God, having full confidence that he will answer. And then, let us humbly accept the guidance he offers."

Frankie jotted the Bible verse down in her bulletin. She would have to give that some thought. She'd gone through a lot of trials in the past year. Had she become more patient, or stronger in her faith because of them? Had she received God's wisdom, and acted on it? She wasn't sure, but she hoped so…

After mass, Tracy had a surprise for her. "I've been working so much I haven't seen anywhere near enough of you. I thought

I'd make it up to you with a day at the conservatory. We could tour the gardens, and there's a butterfly exhibit I think you'd enjoy. We can have dinner in the city later. Would you like that?"

She was sure that flowers and butterflies were not at the top of Tracy's personal to-do list, and the idea that he'd planned such a day just for her made her fall even more in love with him.

The afternoon was steeped in sunshine, and as they strolled through the conservatory's parks and gardens, Frankie felt blessed beyond belief. She was glad she'd thought to stop home and get her camera. There were so many lovely color combinations, so many pretty flowers she'd love to try in her own yard next summer. Maybe Lilly could identify them from the photos.

The center lawn was dominated by a large white gazebo, smothered in cascading pink roses. The space was enchanting, the perfect pace for a wedding, and Frankie wondered if they opened it up to the public.

She could see it so clearly, herself in a white lacy gown, her bridesmaids, Rhoda and Lilly, in palest pink. Tracy in a black tuxedo. It would be the wedding she'd always dreamed of. Maybe it was too early in the relationship to be thinking such things, but she knew how she felt. And how she felt was head over heels in love with Tracy Johanson.

When Alonzo proposed to her, he made it clear he wanted their wedding to be a small affair, that twenty minutes of a judge's time at City Hall would suit him just fine. He'd been married briefly in his thirties, and said he didn't care to have an audience this time around.

His attitude disappointed her. She had been looking at bridal magazines for months, tentatively planning a wedding for a hundred guests, which would cover her few friends, Alonzo's side of the family, and the entire Ragazzo clan. She'd dreamed of wearing a beautiful gown, of lovely music, hand-written vows, and a church overflowing with flowers. He'd made her feel foolish about those dreams, saying she was thirty years old, for heaven's sakes. As if beautiful weddings were only for brides in their twenties.

Her mother wouldn't hear of Frankie getting married at City Hall. She'd insisted on a church wedding, so Alonzo had conceded that point. In the end it had been he and Frankie, his parents and hers, and a priest. A single vase of mixed flowers had decorated the altar, and she'd carried a spray of pink sweetheart roses.

She thought of that day with sadness, but no longer with anger. It was the beginning of a twenty-year imprisonment with Alonzo as her jailer. If she'd stood her ground and gone ahead with her plans for the wedding of her dreams would things have turned out differently?

Without thinking, she blurted, "This would be a beautiful place for a wedding."

Tracy looked surprised. "Yes, it would. For someone."

It was as if he'd thrown a bucket of ice water on her fantasy. She'd spoken without thinking, as usual, and now she felt ashamed. But at least she knew now that he wasn't thinking along the same lines as her. Maybe it was too soon. She didn't know the appropriate time line, all she knew was her own heart. She was embarrassed to have been so transparent, though. When would she ever learn to keep her big mouth shut?

"Come on," he said, taking her hand. "Let's go inside and find your butterflies."

The water garden was a tropical wonderland, a hushed haven with waterfalls and fish ponds and exotic flowering plants and trees. Hundreds of butterflies in all sizes and colors flew freely above and all around them. It was magical, and she felt her earlier disappointment melting away. When a large black and gold monarch landed on her hand, she smiled at Tracy as brightly as if he'd caused it to happen.

"This place is wonderful. I wish we could stay here forever." He drew her to him and kissed her, and in that moment, she felt like a butterfly herself. Free and beautiful, soaring at the top of the world. The memory of that kiss would be the bright spot, the memory to which she returned again and again to help her make it through the week.

•

The next morning, on the seventeenth of August, she walked into Holy Child Academy, determined to enjoy her new job, no matter what. The kids would not start until the following day, and she wanted to get as much prepped for her first lunch of the year as she could.

She'd been meticulous with her menu plans and supply lists for the month, had made copies of the spread sheets and left them in Chelsea's mailbox the week before. She hadn't heard anything back from Chelsea, so supposing no news was good news, she'd gone ahead and placed her first order.

She found Scat waiting for her outside the cafeteria door.

"Good morning!" she said brightly. "Welcome to the new school year."

"Morning," he said sleepily. She unlocked the door and he followed her inside.

The supplies were stacked on pallets in the kitchen area. "I guess our first order of business will be to put these things away. The cold items should be arriving later this morning. I emptied out the coolers and the cupboards last week and scrubbed them all down, so we're starting with a clean slate. Between the two of us, hopefully we can come up with a system that makes sense."

"Cool."

Armed with utility knives, they cut through the packaging and began stacking the items on the counters. They arranged all of the canned goods by categories on the shelves and were deciding on the best place to store the paper products when Chelsea entered the kitchen. She had the copies of Frankie's menu plans in her hand.

"I was at conferences most of last week, so I didn't have a chance to look at these until last night. I wish I'd seen them before you placed the order. I've had to make some changes. We can't serve these fattening meals to the students."

Frankie felt like she'd been slapped.

"This is all carbs and sugars," Chelsea said, tossing the meal plans onto the counter. "You need to think fruits and veggies."

"I added those things as side dishes," she explained. "Teenaged boys can't fill up on apples and carrot sticks."

Chelsea sighed a long-suffering sigh. "Look, Frankie,

things have changed in the years since you went to school. It's all about nutrition now, and the fewer calories the better. I'm sure you're aware of the childhood obesity rate in this county. Things have got to change, and this is where it starts. So let's do it my way, shall we?"

Frankie picked up the menu plans and scanned them. They were a red-ink, scribbled-up mess. Chelsea had changed almost everything Frankie had done. She'd written the word *No!* beside Frankie's signature dishes, her lasagna and Johnny Marzetti.

The students at St. Sebastian's had loved those lunches. Yes, times had changed. Frankie was aware of that every single day. But good food hadn't. Chelsea clearly thought Frankie was too old to do the job. Maybe she was right. She blinked back tears, determined not to cry.

"What's wrong with pasta once a week?" she asked.

"Carbs and sugar, as I said."

Glancing at the ruined plans, she looked at some of Chelsea's substitutions and found them utterly ridiculous. Veggie salad with a side of cherry tomatoes and hummus. Tuna and chick pea pita sandwiches with fresh kiwi and raspberry fruit cups. Chicken avocado pizza.

Keeping her tone steady, she said, "I always tried to incorporate fresh vegetables at St. Sebastian's whenever I could. But Frankly, I don't see how I can serve these lunches and stay on point with the budget I've been given."

Chelsea's eyes narrowed. "St. Sebastian's. They closed that, didn't they, for lack of funding?"

"Yes, they did."

"We're a little more financially sound here, at Holy Child. I'll see what I can do with the budget. Meanwhile, see what you can do to revamp this month's menus."

As she turned and walked out, Scat turned to Frankie. "Wow, that was cold."

Once again, Frankie fought tears. "I'll have you put rest of these things away. Do whatever makes sense to you. I need to go and rewrite my menus."

She ended up staying at work much later than she'd planned. When she got home, the kittens rushed to greet her.

Sugar lay on her blanket, her stubby tail wagging. Frankie noticed she hadn't eaten any of the food or drank the water she'd put out for her that morning.

"Do you not like my food choices either?" she asked, scratching the dog's ears. "Or were you just lonely?" She took Sugar out to the front porch for some fresh air. The dog lay beside her, uninterested in the chipmunks that scurried around the yard.

"You're not sick are you, girl?" she worried.

By evening, Sugar still wouldn't eat, and Frankie decided to call the vet first thing in the morning. She'd see if she could take her in after work.

Chapter Seventeen

The next morning Frankie woke up more determined than ever to prove herself at Holy Child. There wasn't much she could do about the menus she'd planned for the month, but if Chelsea could get her a bigger budget, she'd rise to the challenge and prepare the meals she'd asked for next month. When she arrived at work Scat was waiting for her outside the cafeteria door.

"Good morning, Scat. We'll have to see about getting you your own key."

"Hey, Ms. Bonetti. I don't mind waiting. I'm not on the clock until eight anyway."

She unlocked the door and he hobbled in behind her.

"What did you do to your ankle?"

"I put my foot through a rotted board on the stairs last night. I twisted it pretty good."

"That's terrible. Did you tell your landlord?"

"Ahh, no."

"Have you been to see a doctor?"

"I can't afford that. I'll be fine in a couple of days. What do you want me to do this morning?"

"I was going to have you start prepping vegetables for a salad." She slid a chair over to a low table in the corner. "Why don't you work over here? You can put your foot up on this other chair. I'll go and get the veggies."

While Scat peeled carrots and chopped green peppers, Frankie put her lasagna noodles on the stove to boil. It was a sin, she thought, what health care had come to anymore. Poor Scat. He glanced up and saw her watching him, and she smiled.

"Have you lived in Port Arthur a long time, Scat?"

"Most of my life. I spent a few months in Florida though. I just got back a few weeks ago."

She laughed. "Florida, huh. And you came back north for the winter?"

He shrugged. "It's home."

She got a container of ricotta cheese out of the cooler and mixed her spices into it. "Are you looking toward a career in food service?"

"Nah. This is just something to do for now. I actually want to be a journalist."

"Really?"

He shrugged. "It's just a dream of mine. I'd like to travel, maybe write feature stories for magazines. It would be nice to be my own boss."

"Wouldn't it, though?"

She was going to question him farther, but at that moment Chelsea walked in, her face looking like a thunder cloud. She glanced at the marinara can, and then at Frankie's noodles boiling on the stove. "I thought we agreed we weren't going to serve lasagna."

"Since I'd already bought all of the supplies, I couldn't see wasting them."

Her gaze fell on Scat. "Why is he sitting down?"

Frankie reminded herself to stay calm. To be forgiving. It was a new day. "I told him to. Was there something you needed, Chelsea?"

"Yes, there is. I discovered that the new aide we hired has forty-five minutes of down-time in her schedule on Tuesdays and Thursdays from eleven thirty to twelve fifteen. I'm going to have her come in here and help you two serve on those days. I just wanted to make you aware of it."

"Okay, thanks." She returned to the stove and stirred her noodles, turning her back on Chelsea. When she turned again, the other woman was gone.

Lunch was to be served in three stages, with kindergarten through second grade being served at eleven, third and fourth grades at eleven thirty and fifth through eighth grades at noon.

The first round of lunches went well. Frankie had always had a soft spot for the little ones, and the little ones at Holy Child were cute beyond belief. They came through the line as solemn as little monks, and she knew their teachers had given them the standard "first day of school" lecture on lunchroom procedures and expectations.

She smiled at each one as she served up their lasagna, and began the long process of committing their names to memory. The third and fourth graders were a bit more exuberant, but no less cute. As she took a moment to chat with each one of them, she remembered why she was there in the first place and vowed not to let Chelsea get under her skin any more.

By noon, when the older kids came through the line, Lainey had still not shown up. Frankie smiled at the students' expressions of delight when they saw her lasagna. She also noticed that much of the veggie salad Chelsea insisted she add had gone uneaten.

When the students had settled into their seats at the tables, she smiled at Scat. "Looks like we planned it about right. There might be enough for second helpings, if not too many of them want them. Why don't you get yourself a plate and sit down."

"You sure?"

"Absolutely. You've been on your feet for an hour, serving lunches. You should sit down and put your foot up again."

Scat took the tray of lasagna she offered him and went back to the work table. She noticed that he finished his meal in seconds. She'd just started filling the sink with water when she heard an uproar out in the dining room. Peeking out the serving window, she gasped.

There was a food fight going on.

Carrots and peppers and slices of bread sailed through the air. Pristine white shirts were spattered with marinara sauce. One girl had a piece of lasagna mashed into her hair. Everyone was screaming and nothing she saw made any sense. Good Lord!

"Scat, call Tony's office and ask him to come down here right away!" she said, hurrying into the dining room.

She tried to get control of the situation, and failed miserably. Her voice was completely drowned out by the clamor. The uproar grew louder as the food flew faster. Her stomach squeezed and she felt as though she might be ill. Never, in thirty years at St. Sebastian's, had she dealt with a scenario like this.

"Enough!" Tony Argenteri's voice thundered through the cafeteria as he stood in the doorway, Chelsea beside him. Silence fell among the tables. "What on earth are you kids thinking?"

No one spoke. For a long moment, no one breathed.

"I don't know who is responsible for this, but this is not the way we behave here."

The students sat, some in tears, some hiding smirks, as Tony Argenteri read them the riot act. "For whoever started this, the consequences are going to be mighty," he said. "Ms. Regal and I will be waiting in my office for that person or persons to come forward. If no one does come forward, you will all share the punishment."

A wave of protest rippled through the cafeteria. "Now I want you, all of you, to apologize to Ms. Bonetti. And then I want every last crumb cleaned up off this floor before you go back to class. Understood?"

"Yes, Sir," they said in unison.

"I'll be in my office then. If no one comes to see me by the end of the day, every one of you will have after-school detention every day next week."

The students got busy picking up vegetables and bread crusts. Each one of them apologized to Frankie, eyes cast down, on their way out the door.

Chelsea had stayed behind to supervise the cleanup. When the last student left, she turned to Frankie and Scat. "How did this even happen?"

"I don't know," Frankie said honestly. "We'd just finished serving. I turned my back to run a sink full of water, and next thing I knew …" she raised her hands in a gesture of helplessness.

"And where were you, exactly?" she asked Scat.

"He was helping me with the cleanup," Frankie said. Scat glanced at her, his face betraying surprised relief.

"And where is Lainey?" she demanded.

"I don't know, Ma'am," Scat said.

"Did she not come down and help serve today?"

"No, Ma'am."

She frowned. "Okay. From now on, Scat, I want you to stay out front until the last class leaves."

"No problem."

"When the two of you get this dining room cleaned up, I'd like to see you both in my office." She turned on her high heels and marched from the cafeteria.

"Great," Frankie said. "Just marvelous."

"Thanks for covering for me," Scat said.

"You're welcome."

•

When they'd wiped the tomato sauce from the walls and tables and set the dining room in order, Frankie and Scat headed to the office. Just as Frankie was about to knock on the door, it opened. Lainey brushed past her, eyes red from crying.

"Uh-oh," Scat said softly.

Frankie walked into the office, while Scat stood in the doorway.

"Good times," Chelsea said sarcastically. "Looks like our girl just quit."

"She quit?" Frankie said. "Why?"

"She said she forgot to report to the cafeteria. She smells like cigarettes, so I'm assuming she went out for a smoke break instead. If we'd had an extra set of eyes in there today, maybe the food fight wouldn't have happened. I mentioned that to her. She got upset and quit on the spot."

Frankie shuddered, imagining the scenario. It must have been like a tiger tearing into a scared little rabbit. That poor girl.

"Two boys came forward and admitted to starting the food fight, by the way. I've given them out- of- school suspension for all of next week."

"Out of school? That seems a little extreme."

"I want to send a clear message. That kind of foolishness will not be tolerated at Holy Child Academy. Scat, I'd like to expand your hours to five days a week instead of three. You'll come in at eight o'clock and help with food prep, as usual, but I want you to stay until the last students leave. That will give you an extra ten hours a week without putting you over thirty, which will be perfect. Frankie, after you finish serving, I want you to try and keep a better eye on the room. Walk around, let them know you're the one in charge."

She had always had a great rapport with the kids at St. Sebastian's. There was never any question of who was in charge of the lunch room. She hadn't needed to patrol like a drill sergeant and she hated the idea. "I'll do my best."

"That's all we can ask." Chelsea turned back to her paperwork, clearly dismissing them.

Back in the kitchen, Scat pulled on his hoodie. "That actually worked out pretty well for me. I'm sorry she's blaming you for today, though. It was just as much my fault as yours. Probably more."

"It wasn't anybody's fault. It was just a bunch of kids making unwise choices."

"It was crazy unwise." He laughed. "Did you see the kid with the tomato sauce all down the front of his pants?"

"I guess I missed that." She smiled for the first time since the food fight began. "Why don't you let me give you a ride home? You can barely walk on that ankle."

"Nah. It's not far."

"Well, I'm going out for a little ride anyway. I haven't had my break yet, and I could use a change of scenery for a bit."

She'd driven about four blocks when Scat pointed out a three-story brick building. "It's that one, but don't pull up front. Pull in the alley behind it."

Her glance skimmed over the decrepit building. "Here?"
"I don't want the cops to catch on that there are people living here. They'll run us off."

She gaped at the defunct hardware store with two floors of apartment above it. The building was littered with graffiti, half of its windows broken, the other half boarded up. Along the upper floors, verandas hung crookedly from the building, strewn with people's abandoned possessions; dirty mattresses, broken screens, a child's deflated beach ball.

White notices were taped to every window that wasn't broken.

"Scat, this building is condemned."

"It's better than sleeping under a bridge. Anyway, it's just for a little while, till I can save up a few paychecks and get something better."

Frankie gave the building another once-over. Anything would be better than this. It was no wonder he'd hurt himself falling through the floor. This place was a disaster waiting to happen.

"The City will probably knock this down soon anyway," he said, as if reading her thoughts.

A flash of movement in a second- story window got her attention and she glanced up and saw a woman leaning out. Her steely gray curls peeked out from beneath her white bandanna. She wore a faded Lula Roe blouse. Frankie stared in disbelief. Lilly?

Their eyes met for a fraction of a second and then Lilly quickly pulled her head back inside.

She sat for a moment, staring up at the window, stunned. Should she go in? She really had to get back to work, and Lilly clearly hadn't wanted Frankie to see her. Things were starting to make sense now.

Oh, poor Lilly!

Her mind began to race. What should she do? She had an appointment to take sugar to the vet at four o'clock, and at five thirty she was meeting Tracy for supper. But maybe she'd come back tomorrow and talk to Lilly.

"Thanks for the ride, Ms. Bonetti. I'll see you tomorrow."

"You bet."

With a last glance at the awful building she turned around and drove out of the alley.

She left work at three thirty and hurried home. Sugar barely lifted her head from the blanket, and Frankie noticed she hadn't eaten again. She coaxed her out to the car and by sheer force of will lifted Sugar inside. The dog lay on the back seat, whimpering softly.

The vet took them to an exam room right away. She listened to sugar's heart, looked in her eyes and mouth, and took her temperature. "You said on the phone this dog was abandoned?"

"Yes, that's right."

"Can you tell me anything about her at all?"

"I'm sorry, I can't. I've only had her about three weeks. But she hasn't been herself for the last couple of days. She's not a high- energy dog on a good day, but any more she doesn't even want to get off her blanket."

"I'd say she's around twelve years old, which is about the average life span for the breed. Though I've seen them live as long as fifteen. I don't like what I'm hearing in her bowel area. I'd like to do an X-ray, if that's okay with you?"

"Of course."

Frankie waited what seemed an eternity. Finally the vet tech returned with Sugar, the doctor following with a sleeve of x- rays. She clipped them to a light on the wall. "I'm afraid it's not good news. Do you see this mass here?"

Frankie looked at the ominous blob on the x-ray. "Yes," she whispered.

"This dog has cancer. It's quite advanced."

Frankie sat back, a sensation of numbness creeping over her. "What can we do?"

"Not much at this point, to be honest. This is probably why the previous owners abandoned her."

Frankie buried her face in Sugar's neck. She smoothed the dog's ears with her hands. She couldn't stop touching her, petting her. The vet spoke softly. "She's probably suffering, Ms. Bonetti. I recommend we euthanize."

Tears streamed from Frankie's eyes. "You mean today?"

"She might live another week or two, but it would be a painful life. The tumor is fully engulfing her stomach. She won't be able to eat. Within a day or two, it will start pushing on her lungs, and she won't be able to breathe."

"I understand." She fought to keep herself under control. "Can I have a couple of minutes?"

"Of course. I'll be out front. Let me know when you're ready."

When the door closed behind the vet, Frankie burst into tears. She took out her phone and called Tracy. "Hey, I'm at the vet's office with Sugar."

"All right."

"The thing is, can you come?"

"Sure, I was just finishing up here. Is everything okay?"

"No."

They moved Sugar to a small surgical room and inserted an IV into her leg.

"This is just a sedative," the vet explained. "It will keep her from feeling anxious."

Tracy showed up fifteen minutes later. He walked over to where Frankie sat, cradling the dog, and squatted in front of her. "They told me out front what was happening. I'm sorry, Frankie."

She grasped his hand, clung to it like a lifeline while the vet injected a second medication into sugar's IV. Within moments, she was gone. Frankie held her, tears streaming down her cheeks.

"If you want to go back out front, we'll get her ready for you to take home," the vet said. "Unless you'd like us to dispose of her."

"No, I'm not leaving her here," Frankie croaked.

She paid her bill and went to wait outside. When Tracy came out carrying Sugar's body wrapped in a plastic sheet and put her in the bed of his truck, she could no longer keep it together. She wept bitterly.

Tracy wrapped his arms around her. "I'm so sorry."

It was all too much. The food fight, the constant walking on eggshells with Chelsea, and now, Sugar was gone. Her sweet Sugar. She buried her face in Tracy's chest and sobbed. He held her, stroking her hair and murmuring to her.

"If you'd like, we can take her up to my house and bury her. I've got a big old lilac tree out back I think she'd like. I've buried a couple of my own dogs out there. Unless you want to bury her in your yard?"

"The lilac tree sounds nice. I think she would like that." Fresh tears poured from her eyes. "I know I didn't have her very long... but I loved her."

"Hey," he said gently. "You probably showed that dog more kindness in three weeks than she's known her whole life." He turned her tear stained face up to meet his. "You don't have to know someone for a long time to love them, Frankie."

•

She composed herself enough to drive and followed behind Tracy as he led the way to a large, white colonial on the edge of town. She'd never been to Tracy's house before. It was an older home, not fancy, but well-tended and welcoming.

He got a shovel from the garage and handed it to her to carry while he retrieved the dog from the back of the truck. Beneath the shade of an enormous, fifty-year-old lilac tree, they laid Sugar to rest.

"Let me take a quick shower," he said, "And then I'll see what I can find for us to eat."

"I'm really not hungry."

"You should try to eat, though. I'm sure you haven't had anything since lunch."

She realized then that between the food fight and seeing Lilly in that awful building she hadn't even had lunch.

"Okay."

While Tracy went upstairs to shower, Frankie looked around the house. It was a standard issue single man's home. No frills, no feminine touches. She'd hoped for a glimpse into his past life, but there were no pictures at all. Not of Tracy, Joanne, or Dalton. It was as if he'd swept his home clean of their memories.

He returned to her, freshly showered and shaved. "This place needs a little work, as you can see. The contractor's house is a bit like the shoemaker's kids with no shoes."

"I think it's lovely."

He took two steaks from the refrigerator. "I'll put these on the grill. It won't take a minute."

She found the makings for a tossed salad and put it together while Tracy grilled the steaks. They sat on his back deck and ate them. It was quiet at Tracy's place, peaceful. As if they were miles from the city limits, rather than just two short blocks.

After they'd eaten, they stacked their dishes in the dishwasher and carried their cups of coffee out to the deck.

Her gaze wandered to the lilac tree.

"You okay?" he asked.

"Yeah. I'm just… I'm having a hard week."

He reached across the table and squeezed her hand. "I know."

"I got called to the principal's office today."

"What?"

"It was pretty humiliating. Some of the kids started a food fight. Chelsea's suspending them for a whole week."

"Yikes. Their parents will love that."

"I think she'd suspend me too, if she could. And as I was going into the office, a little teacher aide that just got hired was leaving in tears. The woman is a monster."

"She sounds like a control freak."

"She's the poster child."

"I'm sorry, Frankie. And then to have to put Sugar down on top of all that."

"It's been a little more than I can take. Father Joe's message is a tall order this week."

"Refresh my memory."

"Count it all joy. I don't think I know how to do that right now."

He regarded her thoughtfully. "You really take those messages to heart, don't you?"

"I try to. I mean, what's the point of going to mass if you're just going to take up space in a pew? I feel like if I don't come away different, there's no point in going at all."

"I wish I was more like that."

While they'd talked, darkness had fallen and she hadn't even noticed. "I should probably go home. The cats are probably wondering about their supper, and we both have to work in the morning."

He followed her to her to car.

"Thanks for coming to be with us today and for the lilac tree. I appreciate it."

"I'm here for you." He kissed her forehead, her nose, and her lips. "Any time you need me."

It wasn't until she drove away from him that she let herself think about what he'd told her earlier. *You don't have to know someone for a long time in order to love them, Frankie …*

She turned it over in her mind, wondering if he'd really said what she thought she'd heard.

Chapter Eighteen

On Wednesday morning Frankie headed to work, her determination severely dampened. She felt as wrung out as an old dishrag. She had no aspirations today of impressing anyone or of proving herself. She only hoped to make it through her work day.

Her troubled thoughts scrambled back and forth in her brain. What was she going to do about Lilly? Should she go back to the abandoned building and talk to her, or wait for Lilly to come to her? As often as her thoughts returned to her friend, her silent prayer went up to heaven. *God, what should I do? Please give me wisdom...*

The day passed blessedly uneventfully. The students ate their lunches quietly, without so much as a single pea being thrown. She'd made them a chocolate cake for desert, even though Chelsea would have a fit, to show them there were no hard feelings.

"You're making them cake?" Scat asked, when he saw her assembling the ingredients that morning. "After what they did yesterday?"

"They were just being kids, Scat."

"You know something, Ms. Bonetti? You're good stuff."

If she was good stuff, she thought later, she would have gone to see Lilly on her lunch break. She would have settled the issue once and for all. She'd almost made up her mind to stop at the decrepit old building after work, but a check of her phone showed two missed calls, one from Tracy, and the other from Sal DeFranco.

She hurried home where she could return the calls in

private. Oh, how she wanted to talk to her old friend, to hear a familiar voice, and to have someone to reassure her of her ability to do her job.

She fed the cats, carefully avoiding the empty blanket in the corner. She would have to pack up Sugar's things and put them away, but not today. She didn't have the heart. After making herself a cup of coffee, she took her cell phone out of her purse and returned Sal's call. He answered on the first ring.

"Hey, I've been wondering about you," he said. "The last we talked you'd just moved into a new house. How's that going?"

"The house is wonderful, Sal. I'm really starting to make some headway with the improvements."

"Excellent. And I assume the new job has started?"

She sighed. "Yes."

"You sound less than thrilled."

It was so comforting to hear his voice, to know he would understand the dynamics of the situation, that she spilled the whole story about Chelsea, the food fight, and the ridiculous menu plans.

He laughed. "Are you kidding me? Tuna and chick pea sandwiches?"

"I wish I was, Sal."

"She does sound a little overzealous, but hang in there. She'll settle down."

"Do you think so?"

"I've seen it before, Frankie. New administrators like to try and throw their weight around. Often I think they're more intent on proving something to themselves than anything else. Do you want me to put in a call to Tony, just feel him out, maybe mention again how lucky they are to have you?"

"Oh, no! I wouldn't want you to do that. I appreciate it, but I have to sort this out for myself. I don't remember it being this hard to settle into St. Sebastian's. Of course, that was a lot of years ago."

"You're the best food service director there is, kiddo, and they are lucky to have you. Don't forget that for even a minute." They talked for another half hour and she hung up the phone, feeling better. Sal had always had a way of helping her put things into perspective. He'd helped her to see that she and Chelsea were both new kids on the block at Holy Child. Chelsea just had a different way of handling that than Frankie did. She would try to be patient and overlook the insults. She would try to count it all joy, and in the end, she hoped her faith would come out stronger.

Pouring another cup of coffee, she listened to Tracy's voice mail. "Hey, Frankie, just wanted to see how you were feeling today. Also, I forgot to tell you last night that Rhoda's planning a birthday party for our mother at the nursing home on Sunday. She'll be eighty. If you don't want to go, I completely understand. But can you help me think of what I might be able to get her as a gift? I'm kind of stumped. I'm heading to Chillicothe to pick up a load of roofing tiles right now, but call me later, okay?"

She smiled. She'd suggest a nice bouquet of flowers, her go-to gift idea whenever she was stumped. What better way to cheer up a nursing home, and to say 'I love you' at the same time? She took a sip of coffee, savoring its robust flavor. She couldn't imagine not going to the party. She loved Tracy's family. And it would be nice to meet Tracy's mother, even if she wouldn't remember it.

Lilly weighed heavily on her mind all week, but it was Friday before Frankie finally got up the nerve to stop and see her. She knew what she wanted to do now, what she felt God would have her do. She only hoped Lilly would go along with it. Pulling into the alley, she looked up at the window where she'd seen her last time. Was she imagining it, or did she again detect a slight movement up there?

Locking the car, she slunk in the side door, immediately covering her nose. The stench of mildew and unwashed bodies was overwhelming. She looked around as her eyes adjusted to the dim light.

The building was even worse inside than out. Plaster fell in hunks from the ceiling and the entire floor was strewn with garbage. Along a side wall, mailboxes overflowed with years-old letters and yellowing penny savers.

Picking her way to the staircase, Frankie nearly stepped on a syringe. *That does it*, she thought. One way or another, I'm getting Lilly out of here. Today!

She crept cautiously up the stairs, mindful of the rotting boards. She estimated Lilly's room would be behind one of the doors at the end of the hallway. Taking a calming breath, she knocked softly on the last door in the hallway. There was no answer, but she sensed that Lilly was in there, waiting.

With a light push, the door creaked open. "Lilly?" she said cautiously.

She sat in a beat-up chair by the window, or what was left of one. Stuffing fell out of its arms and seat by the handful. A cot with a thin mattress was neatly made up with a faded and threadbare blanket, Lilly's red wagon parked beside it. A bar of soap and a toothbrush sat in a cup on the floor. Her clothes hung along the wall above the cot. The sight of them hanging neatly from their nails nearly broke Frankie's heart.

"I thought I told you not to come here." Her tone was stiff, icy. She'd never heard Lilly sound that way before.

"I noticed you in the window the other day, and I—"

"I noticed you, too. And did I invite you up?"

"No."

"But you came anyway."

Oh dear. This was not going well at all.

"As long as I'm here, can I talk with you for a few minutes?"

"I don't see how I can stop you."

"Lilly," she said gently, "I'm sure you know that this place is not safe. It's not safe for many reasons."

"You don't like it, then leave."

She was flabbergasted by the coldness in Lilly's tone. She'd known her friend was proud, but she'd never known her to be rude before. This wasn't the Lilly she knew at all.

"I'd like it if you'd come home with me."

"No."

"Just for a while, until we figure something out?"

"It's already figured out. This is my life. This is who I am."

"It doesn't have to be."

"Yes it does." Anger flashed in her eyes. "You think I like living this way? You think I like taking my baths in the sink at the gas mart? Eating canned peaches and dry tuna fish 'cause I ain't got the luxury of a stove or even electricity? You think I like coming up to the rich side of town on garbage day, picking along the curb for things to bring back here and sell? It's a sin what you people throw away!"

"Us people?"

"That's right. You and me, our worlds are worlds apart."

"I wouldn't say that. I think the two of are actually a lot alike."

"Right. We're two peas in a big ol' pod. Well you just go on home to your pod, Frankie Bonetti, and leave me to mine, 'cause I'm not willing to be one of your strays. Your latest Catholic Charity."

The words slammed into her like a fist in the stomach. "I can't believe you would say that to me."

Lilly turned her face to the window.

"I didn't know where you lived. I didn't care where you lived." Her voice cracked. "I never thought of you as a charity. I never thought of you as anything but my friend."

"It was better when you didn't know. Then I could almost kid myself that we was real friends. But now I can see it all up in your face. Disgust. Pity."

"No, Lilly. That isn't true. You're seeing something that's not there."

Her tone became softer, more tired. "If you're my friend, then please go. Go away and stop shaming me."

Frankie left the building in tears. How could she help her friend if she wasn't willing to be helped? Lilly had been her first friend in Port Arthur, had become her dear friend. At least she'd thought so. Losing that friendship was as painful as losing a limb. One she couldn't ever replace. She'd meant to do the right thing, and she'd done the wrong thing after all. Again. When would she ever learn the difference?

Driving away, she swiped at her tears with her hand. Across Cleveland Avenue, a girl on a bicycle weaved in and out between the slow moving cars.

Her long blonde hair whipped across the backpack on her shoulders. A fleeting, unsettling impression made Frankie glance in her rearview mirror.

There was something about the girl that reminded her of Allie. But that was crazy. Allie wouldn't be over here, in this neighborhood. Would she? She shot another hard glance in the mirror, but by then the girl was too far away to see.

Chapter Nineteen

Frankie thought surely Lilly would think things over, that she would come by the house and they would sit on the porch and talk the whole thing out. But Saturday slipped away with no sign of her.

On Sunday after church, she and Tracy stopped at the supermarket on their way to the nursing home. Perusing the flower displays, Tracy selected an arrangement of bright yellow and red lilies. "This will be perfect," he said. "Thanks for the idea. I was fresh out. I think she's got all of the bath robes she can use."

Frankie smiled.

"She always loved flowers, and these will make her room more cheerful. And thanks for going with me."

"I wanted to, Tracy. I'm looking forward to meeting your mother."

"You won't meet my mother," he said. "She's been gone a long time. I only hope the party makes her happy."

Leaving the store, she noticed the wistful smiles of the other women they passed. Their eyes moved from Frankie to the beautiful flower arrangement and then skimmed over Tracy. She understood the jealousy she saw on their faces all too well. She'd worn it herself, many years ago. Tracy was so good looking, so good to be with that she still had to pinch herself to make sure he was really a part of her life.

Winding Trails Nursing Facility sat on the north end of Jackson Place, a pretty little cul-de-sac on the outskirts of town. From the outside, the two-story whitewashed building looked like a cheerful retreat, with its windows trimmed in red, white window boxes spilling nasturtiums and red petunias. Inside, though, she saw that it was the same combination of disinfectant and despair that characterized nursing homes everywhere.

In the activities room, a banquet table had been set with gold balloons and table cloths of midnight blue. A large cake sat in the center, flanked on either side by a punch bowl and stacks of blue and gold plates and cups. Rhoda and Guy stood talking with some of the staff members while a handful of senior citizens dozed in wheel chairs along the wall.

"Welcome to the party," Rhoda greeted them, kissing them each on the cheek. There was no mistaking the tension behind her smile.

"How long have you been here?" Tracy asked.

"Not long. Maybe twenty minutes. "

"Hey, you two." Guy's smile seemed forced as well.

Tracy greeted him, then glanced around the room. "Where's Allie?"

"Well, now, that's the question of the hour. She took off on her bike this morning and didn't get back in time to come with us. When I try to call, all I get is voice mail."

Tracy's brow furrowed. "That's not like her."

Rhoda let loose a short, angry bark of laughter. "It's all too like her, these days. Will you try and call her, Trace? She might pick up for you."

"Sure. Let me introduce Frankie to Mom first."

He led Frankie to a recliner, where a frail looking, white-haired woman slept. Leaning in close, he spoke softly in her ear. "Happy birthday, Mom. Look, I brought you some flowers."

He set the arrangement on the end table beside her.

She opened her eyes and stared at him with a blank expression.

"This is my friend, Frankie. She came to help us celebrate."

"Hello, Mrs. Johanson."

"Her name's Rita."

"Hello, Rita."

Rita didn't respond or even seem to notice Frankie was there. Frankie took her hand and sat beside her while Tracy went outside to make his phone call. She stroked Rita's hand as her glance moved to the line of people along wall. She looked at each faraway face and wondered who they'd been before time had stolen their identities. It was depressing. She was glad she'd never had to see her mother in a nursing home.

Frankie had been married for two years when her father died of heart failure at age seventy-seven. After her husband's funeral, Irene Ragazzo had stopped eating.

She took off her coat, laid down in her bed, and never got back up. No amount of coaxing could get even her favorite foods down her. She lost weight until she simply disappeared. Her sister, Frankie's Aunt Maxine, had spent the next few weeks helping Frankie care for Irene at home.

Six months after her father died, Frankie's mother slipped away in her sleep. Thought she and her mother had never been close, Frankie didn't think she couldn't have borne a slow disappearing act that lingered year after year, and she felt sorry for Tracy and Rhoda to have to see Rita this way.

When Tracy returned, Rhoda hurried over to him. He must have gotten ahold of Allie, because the look of relief on Rhoda's face was obvious even from where Frankie sat. With a last pat of Rita's hand, she stood and walked over to them.

"So she says she's with a friend, and will head over here right now," Tracy told Rhoda.

"Honestly Tracy, I'm at my wit's end with that girl anymore."

"Just all of a sudden, she's changed that much?"

"It's been building for a few weeks. Little things. She's secretive. I mean she's always been that way with me, but she'll usually open up to Guy. Not this time. And I found out she's cut her last period study hall twice in three weeks and yesterday she didn't go to twirling practice. That worries me more than anything else. She's wanted to be a twirler ever since she saw her first parade. When I asked her about it, she said the parades were boring, that she'd rather hang out with a friend."

"A boy, you think?" Tracy asked.

"I'd bet my life on it."

It was then that Frankie remembered seeing the blonde girl

on the ten speed. She didn't dare mention it to Rhoda, since she didn't get a good look at the girl's face. It might not have been Allie at all. But maybe she would mention it to Tracy later, just in case it was.

"I'll talk to her, Rhodie. See what I can find out for you."

"Will you, Trace? I'd feel a lot better."

The party was a small, sad affair and Rita slept through most of it. Eventually Allie arrived and the atmosphere went from depressing to downright stressful. Tracy was subdued when he took Frankie home that afternoon and she guessed the reasons were twofold.

"Do you want to come in for a while?" she asked.

He turned off the engine. "Sure."

He sat on the couch and the kittens immediately came and swirled around his feet. "You look worn out."

"It takes a lot out of me, seeing her like that. I wish you could have known her back in the day. She was quite a woman."

She sat down beside him and took his hand. "Tell me about her."

He was quiet for a long moment, then said, "Me, my dad, Rhoda … We were her world.

"When dad was alive she mostly stayed home with us. It was the 'sixties. It was what women did then, I guess. But two weekends a month she'd go and sit with an old lady. She'd do her housework, make sure she took her medicine, things like that. She saved all the money she made so that every summer our family could go to Lake Erie and rent a cabin.

"It was a storybook family vacation. We all lived for that week. Fishing, swimming, cooking over a campfire. Mom loved the bonfires the most. She'd break out the marshmallows and the sticks and we'd all settle in." He laughed softly. "She had a way of telling a ghost story that would keep Rhoda and I awake all night for the rest of the summer."

He picked up Pepper and scratched him behind the ears. "And then my father died, and she had to go back to work full time. She was in the surgical unit at the hospital and it demanded her whole life. She worked seven days a week, most weeks, and we stopped going to the cabin. I was in high school by then anyway and probably thought I was too cool.

But Rhoda really missed it, so mom would try to find other ways to make the summer special. They'd make S'mores in the back yard over the fire pit. I was too old for that, but I'd always find a Hershey's bar under my pillow on those nights.

"After she retired, she and Rhoda started going to the lake again. Just for a weekend each summer. She always wanted me to go. 'Please, Trace, come and sit by the bonfire with us, for old time's sake,' she'd say. But by then I had a business to run. It would have meant so much to her, to have us all back at the cabin. And Dalton would have loved it. But I never quite got around to going."

He sighed. "And then a few years ago I started noticing little things. Little telltale signs that she was losing her memory. I told myself it wasn't happening, because I knew it was, and it scared me to death. I wish I had spent that time with her when I still could. She was a good mother. Sometimes I don't feel like I was a very good son."

"I'm sure you were a wonderful son," Frankie said softly.

He squeezed her hand.

"We all have regrets, Tracy. We're none of us perfect people."

"And now there's this business with Allie. All this stuff Rhoda's saying, it's exactly what I've been worried about. This is exactly how it starts."

"I probably shouldn't say anything," Frankie began. "I saw a girl that could have been Allie over on Cleveland Avenue a couple of days ago."

"On Cleveland Avenue? What was she doing?"

"Riding her bike. It was around four o'clock."

"I don't like that. I don't even like you being over there, let alone Allie."

"I may have been wrong. I was upset."

"Well now I'm upset."

"Maybe I shouldn't have said anything at all."

"No, I'm glad you did. Be sure and let me know if you see her over there again."

•

On Monday after school, Frankie returned to the abandoned building. She was determined to make Lilly see reason this time. This time, no matter what Lilly said, she would not be put off. The answer had come to her while she slept. It was very simple, really.

She'd hire Lilly as a live-in house and yard keeper. She couldn't pay her much, but Lilly would have a safe place to live, a little money in her pocket, and her pride. And Frankie would have her company.

She strode in the side door, walked briskly up the stairs, and knocked on the door at the end of the hallway. She didn't get an answer, but then, she didn't expect one. She pushed the door open and looked around in dismay.

Lilly was gone.

The red wagon, the clothes, the bar of soap and the toothbrush, everything was gone except for the cot and the ruined chair. Her heart sank. Why had she left? So as not to risk another encounter with Frankie?

She crept along the hallway, listening at each door she passed. Behind one, she heard an unsettling scuffling sound, like some sort of animal, and she jumped back in alarm. There could be anything or anyone lurking behind these doors. She left quickly. Canvassing the neighborhood, she kept her eyes peeled for any sign of her friend. After an hour of driving around, she went home, disappointed and frustrated.

On Tuesday morning when Scat came into her office, she questioned him about Lilly.

"Oh yeah, I've seen that lady. I mean, it's not like any of us are what you would call neighborly though. We're all just living our separate lives under the same leaky roof."

"She's my friend, Scat, and I'm concerned for her safety. Do you have any idea where she might have gone?"

"There's lots of empty buildings around, she might have moved to a different one. The only other place I can think of would be Tent City."

"Tent City?"

"It's over in Madison Park, beyond the railroad tracks. Some people have set up tents to live in. Some just sleep on blankets on the ground. The cops don't bother them much, if they stay out of sight. They know people have nowhere else to go."

"Where is this park?"

"It's at the end of Akron Street, but trust me, Ms. Bonetti, you don't want to go over there. It's not a good place."

"I'd like to try and find her, though."

"Let me ask around. Someone might know her."

"You'll let me know if you hear anything?"

"Sure."

"Here, I'll give you my number." She jotted her cell number on a sticky note and handed it to him. "Call if you should ever see her. Day or night.""

"Yeah, okay. Hey, do you mind if I charge my phone?"

"Go ahead."

He pulled a phone and charger out of his pocket and plugged it in on her desk. It was a Straight Talk phone, its cover decorated with glittery Zebra stripes. Frankie stared at the phone, going cold. It looked just like Allie's phone from the Memorial Day party. The one she told her mother she lost. But her imagination must be running away with her. She supposed it was a common enough cover.

But for a twenty-year-old man?

Later, she shot sidelong glances at Scat as they began to pull the day's vegetables from the cooler. Thoughts swirled in her head like autumn leaves in a windstorm. It was hard to keep them collected.

She'd seen Allie on her bike, near Scat's building, a bulging backpack on her shoulders. Bulging with what? Rhoda's food? Now Scat had a phone that looked exactly like one Allie said she'd lost. But this was all just a crazy coincidence, wasn't it? Where would Allie have even met Scat?

As Lilly had said to her, their worlds were worlds apart.

For the rest of the day, a tug-of-war went on inside of her. Scat was a nice kid, but he had to be twenty years old or more. Much too old for Allie. Guy would go through the roof, and she didn't even want to consider what Tracy's reaction would be. Should she confront Scat? But about what, exactly? Having a girlie phone?

God, please, I need wisdom. Please don't let me do the wrong thing again.

She kept herself cool. She would not run ahead this time. This time she would wait until God gave her a sign.

Chapter Twenty

The Foxfire Theater had occupied its place in the center block of Main Street since 1928: a three-story building with red and gold awnings, a glass ticket booth, and white lights twinkling like stars along its ninety-year-old marquis. Tracy had spent most of his Sunday afternoons there, growing up, and too many Saturday nights to count.

The theater had closed its doors in the eighties, when Port Arthur's neighboring cities built multi-cinemas and started offering three movies per night, and the aging Foxfire could no longer compete. It stayed closed for nearly twenty years, until Port Arthur's City Planning Committee had raised funds and secured grants to refurbish the historic building. It reopened as The Foxfire Cultural Arts Center in 2002, and since then it had hosted a variety of traveling theaters, comedy acts, and musical groups.

On Saturday evening Tracy stood in his kitchen, ironing his good white shirt. Tonight the theater was presenting a brass band ensemble. Not particularly his thing, but he thought Frankie might enjoy it. He was worried about her lately. She'd had a rough couple of weeks settling into her new job, and now on top of that, she was tying herself in knots over some homeless woman.

That was Frankie, through and through. A woman whose big, generous heart too often caused her pain. The funny thing was, the things that sometimes made Frankie so exasperating to him were the very things that drew him to her. In any case, he wanted her to have a nice time tonight, and he hoped dinner and evening of music would take her mind off of unpleasant things.

She opened the door before he knocked, like she always did. She smiled, looking so lovely in a wine colored dress, her dark hair caught up in a loose knot, that she took his breath away.

"Is Mama Mia's all right?" he asked.

"Mama Mia's is perfect," she said, as he'd known she would.

He'd always liked the restaurant's authentic Italian cuisine, its pleasant atmosphere, and the fact that it wasn't usually very crowded.

He ordered spaghetti and meatballs because he said she'd spoiled him for anyone else's lasagna. He didn't tell her that she'd spoiled him for anyone else's anything. She gave him that endearing half smile of hers.

"What are you buttering me up for, Tracy Johanson?"

He shrugged. "Can't a guy take his lady out for a nice dinner without being up to something."

At times, like right now, he wanted to take her in his arms and hold on for dear life. Or drop to one knee and beg her to marry him. At other times, he knew that wouldn't be fair. She deserved more than him. So much more.

It was no secret that he was not good at relationships. He'd let his mother down. His own son had stolen from him, and then walked away without looking back. Even Joanne, whom he'd thought of as his soulmate, hadn't trusted him with the truth.

They ate their meal, slipping into easy conversation. He asked her if she'd had any luck finding her friend. She shook her head, her eyes sad, and he wished he hadn't mentioned it. He never wanted to be the one to put that sadness in her eyes. Good Lord, those eyes. He hadn't even known her four months, and he was so deeply in love with her he could hardly function. But when he tried to tell her, the words stuck in his throat.

The theater was air-conditioned and he dropped his arm around her shoulders. She snuggled against him. The musicians, a six piece brass ensemble out of Columbus, were better than he'd imagined they would be. He chanced sideways glances at Frankie and saw that her eyes were shining. Noticing him watching her, she smiled.

"This is so nice, Tracy. Thank you. I needed this today."

When the concert ended, they stayed in their seats and waited for the theater to clear out. He told her about the Sunday matinees, and how his mother would let him sit in the balcony with his friends while she and Rhoda sat in the front row.

"It's absolutely beautiful," she said, her glance sweeping across the gold plated walls and ceiling, the crystal chandelier. "People even rent it for events," he told her. "It wouldn't be a half bad place for a wedding."

"No it wouldn't," she answered, hiding a smile. "For someone."

•

The evening would have been perfect if she wasn't so worried about Lilly. Tracy thought her concern stemmed from old-fashioned, Christian charity. What he didn't understand was that she would never stop looking for her friend. She prayed every day that God would keep Lilly safe.

Every day after work last week she'd driven around the city's back alleys and broken streets, peering into store windows and scrutinizing the people walking past, hoping to catch sight of a red wagon, a faded skirt, a headful of steel gray curls. She would not give up until she found her. She would not stop asking until God gave her a sign.

She'd pulled up a map of Port Arthur online and located Madison Park on Akron Street. She'd driven by every day since then. Just off of the walking path, tucked into a field beside the railroad tracks, she'd found the little community of tents, just as Scat had said. It was early September. Summer's oppressive heat was already giving way to an early fall. What would these people do when winter came?

What would Lilly do?

Every day at work she asked Scat if he'd heard anything.

"No, I'm sorry, Ms. B," he told her every day. "I haven't heard anything at all yet."

She was slowly settling into Hold Child, developing relationships with the students and even some of the teachers. But they were co-workers and acquaintances. None of them were what she would call friends. Not like the friend she'd had in Lilly.

Until she'd ruined everything.

In the third week of September she drove past the hardware store. She always looked, just in case Lilly had come back. So far there was no sign of her. Today, though, she saw something unusual. A glimmer of pink and chrome beside the door. Circling the block, she drove past again, more slowly this time. Her breath caught. There, propped against the wall, sat Allie's ten speed.

Surely it was time to confront them. As clearly as if it had been sprayed on the wall in graffiti, or lit up in neon, surely this was her sign.

She parked her car in a spot in front of the building. She would not hide around back this time. If she attracted attention going inside, so much the better. No one should live in this death trap. She walked in the side door, past the garbage and the mailboxes. Heart pounding, she made her way up the stairs. She walked slowly down the hallway, listening at every door. Behind the third door on the left, she heard the vibration of voices. One deep and male. One higher pitched and female.

Okay, God. Here I go …

Her knock was met with silence.

"Scat?" she called.

She heard a scuffling sound inside, and then frantic whispers. The door opened and Scat stared at her in disbelief.

"Ms. Bonetti?"

"May I come in?"

"Ahh, this is not really a good time."

"I think it's a very good time," she said, using her best no-nonsense cafeteria lady voice.

Sighing, he pushed the door wide. Inside, the room was strewn with dirty clothes and blankets and empty food packaging. Her glance skimmed over the granola bar wrappers, the Captain Crunch cereal boxes. The empty bottles of Pepsi and Gatorade, and the peanut butter jars. Allie's backpack.

And finally, Allie.

"What are you doing here?" the girl demanded.

"I was just going to ask you the same question, Allie."

"We're just talking."

"This is no place for a fourteen-year-old girl to be hanging out. Do you have any idea how upset your mother is with the way you've been acting?"

Allie stared at the floor, not answering.

"Hey, no disrespect, Ms. Bonetti, but this isn't really your business."

"And you," she gave him a pointed glance. "Her father is going to skin you alive."

He laughed softly. "No, he won't."

His laughter infuriated her as much as it frustrated her. "I wouldn't bet on that. And this is not a bit funny. Do you realize you could go to jail?"

Allie giggled nervously.

Surprise registered on Scat's face before a slow realization seemed to dawn on him and he laughed again. "Nobody's going to jail."

"I can understand the attitude from her," she gestured to Allie. "But Scat, I'm amazed that you can't see how serious this is."

"Look, I'm really sorry, Ms. Bonetti, okay? I get how this looks to you, but trust me, it's not like that. It's not what you think at all."

"What is it, then?"

"Allie, she's not my girlfriend." He sighed, ran a hand back through his overgrown curls. "She's my cousin."

•

The house on Grandview Avenue was cursed. Tracy was sure of it. Everything that could have possibly gone wrong with the project did, and then some. After today, it would be in the books. Good riddance, he thought. The crew had finished installing the siding that afternoon. All that was left was to put up the new shutters. He'd just screwed the first one into place when his cell rang.

"What's up, Rho?"

"I'm going to have a nervous breakdown, Tracy. I really am."

His blood pressure kicked up a notch. This would be about Allie, no doubt. "What's wrong?"

"I came to pick Allie up from twirling practice. I had a light day, so I came early thinking I'd watch her practice for a little bit. Trying to show an interest, be a good mother, ya know?"

"Right."

"So here I am, sitting at the middle school, and Allie's not here." Her voice rose to near hysteria, sending his blood pressure skyrocketing. "Tracy I don't know what to do."

"Okay, calm down. Would she have just left early for some reason?"

"They said she didn't come today at all. She dropped out of twirling yesterday. Guy is going to have a fit."

"Okay, go home in case she shows up there. I'll go out and see if I can find her."

"I've called and texted all of her friends. She's not with any of them. Unless they're lying. Why would she do this to me?"

"Rhodie, go home. I'll find her."

Handing the shutters off to Pal, he jumped in his truck. This had to stop. It stressed him out. It frightened him. Because this was how it started, with the secrets and the lying. Was it drugs? *Oh, God. Don't let it be that ...*

Dalton had been just twenty when it started for him. He'd been barely more than a teenager, and Allie ... She was only a child. Kids had no idea the roaring lion they were playing with, how it would tear their lives apart before they even realized they were in its clutches.

He made several passes down Main Street, glancing in the windows of the pizza shops and the arcades. No sign of her. Frankie had said she thought she saw her on Cleveland Avenue one day. Maybe he'd run down there. One thing was for sure. He'd find her if it took all night. And heaven help the boy he found her with.

Four blocks from Holy Child Academy he noticed Frankie's car parked in front of the old Cox Hardware store. *Strange,* he thought.

Why would she be parked on this block? There were no stores, no places of business, only abandoned buildings. Slowing, he shot a glance into the alley. He hit the brakes. Allie's bike was chained to a railing beside the stairs. The ten speed he'd bought for her birthday last year.

He pulled in beside it, his heart gripped by icy fingers of fear.

Opening the door, he stepped inside the building. The squalor was absolute. What were Frankie and Allie doing here? His imagination was in overdrive, conjuring horrible images of Frankie and Allie, murdered by some crazed drug addict. Or worse.

He made a quick pass through the building's lower level, his uneasy glance trained on the ceiling. The building was not only a rat-infested mess, it was structurally unsound. Years of exposure to rain and wind had rotted out the ceiling and floor joists, making the entire structure shift at a precarious angle. It could come down at any moment.

He bolted up the stairs, skirting several rotting boards. Creeping through the dim hallway, he heard voices and hurried toward them. They seemed to be coming from behind the third door on the left. Stopping, he pressed his ear against it and tried to process the sounds he was hearing.

Laughter?

He pounded on the door with his open hand. The laughter stopped. When the door opened, the first thing he saw was Frankie. The second was his son.

Surprise left him momentarily speechless.

"Dalton?"

Allie stepped forward. "Uncle Tracy."

Tracy's eyes swept over the squalor in front of him. It hurt him, to know his son would rather live in this filth than come home and live with him.

"You've been here all this time?"

"No. I've been in Florida. I've only been back home a few weeks."

Home. Pain tore through him, because in his son's dark-shadowed eyes, he could see his failure plainly. His failure as a father.

An avalanche of memories tumbled down around him. He was drowning. Birthday parties and spelling bees. Teaching him how to ride a bike. Driving lessons and football games, and always, always, Joanne there to smooth the tension that had always existed between Tracy and his son. His beloved son, whom he wanted so much for.

He ached to pull him into his arms, to take him home and start again. But Dalton obviously didn't want that. So instead, he said, "So the prodigal returns. But rather than return to his father, he prefers to stay in the swine pit, like a pig."

"Tracy," Frankie said softly. "He doesn't mean it, Scat."

Scat. The name cut him to the bone. Joanne had called him that when he was just a little boy. Images swam in and out of focus, Dalton fresh from the bath, wrapped in a towel. Joanne carrying him down the hall, singing the silly rhyme she'd made up for him.

Scatty Catty out of the bathie.
Scatty Catty, time for the nappie,
but Scattie Catty, you must see your daddy!

A warm, soft body dropped in his lap, giggling.

The memory filled him with pain. And the pain filled him with rage. For all of the lost dreams, the hopes he'd had that life had stolen from him.

He gestured toward Allie. "You should be ashamed of yourself, bringing her into this drug- infested rat hole."

"No Uncle Tracy," Allie protested softly. "It wasn't like that. He never asked me to come here. I came on my own."

"I'm clean, dad."

"Yeah. You look it."

"Tracy, please." Frankie moved toward him. He saw his failure reflected in her eyes and it was more than he could bear. It was the three of them against him, and he felt suddenly beaten. Betrayed.

"You knew about this?" he asked her. "All this time, you knew where he was?"

"No. I didn't."

"Then what are you doing here?"

"I actually thought that … I mean, I knew he was here, but

I didn't—"

"Allie, I promised your mother I'd bring you home. Let's go."

"I'm staying here with Dalton, Uncle Tracy," she said, eyes downcast. "I'm really sorry."

It was three against one. He saw it in their faces. He'd been beaten. Betrayed. He turned and strode away, not looking back when Frankie called his name.

•

Frankie, Scat and Allie stood in stunned silence as the dust settled behind Tracy's slammed door. Then Scat turned to Allie. Frankie could see tears gathering in his eyes. "What did I tell you?"

"He'll come around."

"No he won't."

Frankie's mind worked furiously to find the right words, words that would soothe the boy's pain. Before she could find them, Scat climbed out the window, scrambled down the fire escape, and disappeared into the alley.

"Look what you did!" Allie shrieked. "Why did you even come here? You ruined everything!"

She scrambled down the fire escape after Scat, leaving Frankie alone in the wreckage she'd created.

Chapter Twenty-One

Had she ruined everything? It certainly seemed that way.

The week that followed was the longest of Frankie's life. In the evenings she wandered through her house, every empty room a space that Tracy's hands had touched and brought order to, brought sunlight to. She became obsessed with watching out the window. For what, she couldn't say. Obsessed with checking and double checking a phone that didn't ring.

She'd never known a more desolate time. Her years with Alonzo had been lonely, but not knowing how full or how joyful life could be, she hadn't noticed the emptiness so much. Not like she did now. Now, loneliness was like a gray, drizzling rain she could not find shelter from. She honestly didn't think the sun would ever shine again.

She'd called Tracy for three days, leaving message after message, trying to explain. He wouldn't return her calls. He thought she'd known about Dalton all along. He thought she'd betrayed him, and that was what hurt most of all.

Work became a succession of routine days. Scat had not returned since the conflict and his absence only underscored her feeling of desolation. The mornings were chaotic without his help, but the busy pace helped her to get through the endless days.

On Friday afternoon, a week after the altercation, she was sitting in her office, going over the students' lunch accounts on her laptop, when Chelsea walked in.

"Have you got next week's supply list for me?" she asked.

"Yes, it's right here," she said, handing a folder across the desk.

"So, have you heard anything from your boy?"

"No, I haven't."

"I'm sure he realizes that after a week of no call no show, we won't be able to take him back."

"I'm sure he does."

"I suppose we'll have to run an ad. What a hassle. We shouldn't have hired him in the first place," she muttered.

Frankie looked up from her accounts. "Excuse me?"

"All these low life's Tony always wants to give a chance to. It's ridiculous. They don't want to work. They want everything handed to them."

Anger licked at Frankie's insides at Chelsea's smug tone and her high-and-mighty attitude. Who was she to judge Scat or anybody else?

"Get out," she said.

Chelsea looked at her in utter surprise. "What did you say?"

"Get out of my office."

"I'm going to pretend I didn't hear that."

Frankie glared at her. "I don't care what you pretend."

"You'd better watch your step, Frankie."

"I won't watch my step. Not anymore. I'm tired of your condescending attitude. You're a rude and self –absorbed little woman. You have no regard for anyone else's feelings and I've had enough of it. So unless you've got business in here, please stay out of my office."

She watched, feeling vaguely detached as Chelsea stormed away, her high heels clicking on the cafeteria floor. She would probably lose her job now. She couldn't make herself care.

•

For the first time in her life, Frankie stopped going to mass. On Sunday morning, while the church bells rang, she sat on her porch, wrapped in a blanket, staring down the street.

She'd willfully and utterly disobeyed one of the Ten Commandments, but Monday came, and nothing was different. The earth didn't open and swallow her up, and mercifully, Chelsea stayed away from her. Tuesday stretched into Wednesday, and Wednesday into Thursday. It was a long, empty week. She started checking the online papers in Cincinnati for houses and jobs. She would leave Port Arthur, she decided. She would leave the scene of her crimes and not look back.

On Friday when she arrived home from work, Rhoda's SUV was parked in her driveway. Frankie's first impulse was to drive off quickly and avoid whatever painful things Rhoda had come to say.

But no doubt she'd come to talk with her about Tracy.

Frankie was desperate to hear what she had to say. Pulling in a deep breath, she got out of her car. Seeing her, Rhoda climbed out of the SUV.

" Hi."

"Hi, Rhoda."

"Have you got a few minutes? I was hoping we could talk."

Frankie gestured toward the house and Rhoda followed her inside.

In the kitchen, she automatically made a pot of coffee. When it was ready, she poured two cups and set them on the table. Rhoda reached for one and took a swallow.

"How have you been?" she asked.

"Not very good."

"Frankie, I feel terrible about everything that's happened. Allie told me the whole story. There's so much I want to say to you. I just don't know where to start."

"Tell me about Dalton and Allie."

Rhoda sipped her coffee as she collected her thoughts. "Allie and Dalton, they've always had a special bond. Allie's looked up to him all of her life. He's like the older brother she never had.

After what happened with the money a couple of years ago, when Tracy threw him out, Dalton got arrested on drug charges. Rather than give him more jail time, the judge sentenced him to a year in a Florida rehab center.

He finished the program a few months ago and came home. He wanted to patch things up with Tracy, but he couldn't find the nerve to contact him, so he reached out to Allie instead. She's been trying to fix this mess on her own. Cutting school to take him food. To be his friend. " Tears welled up in her eyes. "She didn't trust Guy and me enough to tell us. She didn't think we'd be on her side. We're still working through it all."

"Do you have any idea where he is?"

"I wish I did. Tracy is a mess. This is killing him."

Frankie took a swallow of coffee, set her cup down, and then picked it up again. "Why is he so angry with me, Rhoda?"

"He's not angry with you. He's angry with himself. You have to understand Tracy. He pushes away the very people he wants and needs the most. And Frankie, right now he needs you. Please don't give up on him."

"I don't want to. I don't ever want to. But I'm afraid he's given up on me."

●

An hour later Frankie slipped in the back door of St. Bridgette's and slowly made her way to the front of the church. She sank to her knees before the statue and gazed up into the Shepherd's loving face.

"God, I know you're there," she began. "I know you've always been there."

Tears flowed from her eyes. "I also know I've made a lot of mistakes. All my life I've tried to do the right thing, but I always seem to end up getting it wrong. I've run ahead of you again and this time I've hurt people I love. Lilly. Scat. Tracy." Her voice cracked. "Please help them to find peace. Help us all to find peace."

Gazing at the statue of Jesus tenderly holding the lamb, the words of an old hymn, Shepherd Lead Us, came to mind. Softly, she sang the parts she could remember, tears coursing down her cheeks. And in the hushed shadows of the altar, she felt hope stir in her heart.

●

Things were back to the way they'd been before he ever knew Frankie Bonetti existed. Except now that he knew, Tracy's life was unbearable without her.

He stopped to pick up a sandwich after work and ate it in the truck on his way home. It was almost nine o'clock and he hadn't eaten since lunch. Rhoda had called earlier to invite him for supper, but he told her he wanted to be alone. Which was the paradox of his life. He couldn't bear to be with other people, and he couldn't bear to be alone with himself.

After that day in the hardware store he'd patched things up with Allie the best he could. If he'd only stopped to listen that day, instead of shooting off his big mouth, he would have understood.

Dalton had come back from Florida to try and straighten things out with him. Instead of hearing what Dalton had to say, he'd gone shooting off like a cannon, leveling everything in his path. Including Dalton. He'd lost his son again. This time maybe for good.

To make matters worse, Frankie had seen a side of him he never wanted her to see. The ugly, angry side he was ashamed of. She'd called for three days, leaving messages, and then she'd moved on. She likely never wanted to see him again and he didn't blame her.

He should move on as well. But how could he move forward, when his heart insisted he go back?

Part Five

Jesus Calms the Storm

Chapter Twenty-two

Frankie walked in the door of St. Bridgette's just as the service began on Sunday morning. She slipped into a pew in the back, hoping to go unnoticed. She didn't want to chat today, or to answer the questions Mary Margaret was sure to ask.

She felt the stares of curious people land on her as she knelt to pray. Ignoring them, she focused on trying to recapture the peaceful, hopeful feeling she'd found at the altar two days before.

The service was lovely.

The prayers seemed more meaningful today and the songs, more beautiful. When the first reader took his place at the ambo she gave him her full attention.

"A reading from the Book of Romans."

"Praise to you, Lord Jesus Christ."

"And we know that all things work together for good to those who love God, to those who are called according to His purpose."

She thought back over all that had happened in the last few weeks and tried to imagine good coming out of it. It was difficult to see how each piece, each fragment of joy and heartache, each misunderstanding fit into a larger, more meaningful plan. She couldn't see it. But she would do her best to believe that it was true.

Her thoughts returned to the altar when Father Joe began to speak.

"Peace be with you."

"And with your spirit."

"A reading from the holy Gospel according to Mark."

"Glory to you, Lord."

"On the same day, when evening had come, He said to them, 'Let us cross over to the other side.' Now when they had left the multitude, they took Him along in the boat as He was. And other little boats were also with Him. And a great windstorm arose, and the waves beat into the boat, so that it was already filling. But He was in the stern, asleep on a pillow. And they awoke Him and said to Him, 'Teacher, do You not care that we are perishing?'

"Then He arose and rebuked the wind and said to the sea, 'Peace! Be still!' And the wind ceased, and there was great calm. But He said to them, 'Why are you so fearful? How is it that you have no faith? And they feared exceedingly, and said to one another, 'Who can this be, that even the wind and the sea obey him?'

"This is the word of the Lord."

"Thanks be to God."

Father Joe paused for a moment, and then said, "Do you think when Jesus told the disciples to cross to the other side of the sea that he knew there was a storm coming? Of course he did. Even so, he instructed them to forge ahead. For you see, our Lord does not promise that if we follow him we will not run into troubles. But he does promise to be with us in life's storms. And to help us overcome them, if we will only put our trust in him. That the apostles' faith wavered reminds us that even those who walk very closely with Jesus sometimes find it hard to be faith-filled. But let us be reminded that just as he was able to calm the storm for the apostles, he is able to rescue us from the storms of everyday life, if we will only put our faith in him. And healing comes when we take that faith, and go on to help others through their storms."

Once again, Father Joe had nailed it.

The last few days had been nothing, if not stormy. But Frankie was going to try and see things in a different way now. She would try to stop relying on herself and trust in God to help her through the storms. Starting today.

Back home, she ate a sandwich, then went out to her garden to cut back her flowers. She'd read an article on how to harvest seeds, so she carefully opened the pods, removed the seeds, and tucked them into envelopes for next year. She would be here, in Port Arthur, in the spring. She would not run back to Cincinnati. There was nothing to return for. She would stay in her new life and make the best of it, make some new friends, maybe eventually start dating again. With or without Tracy. Her heart tore in two. Tracy. Lord, how she loved that man. But did she want a man who didn't love her? At least, didn't love her enough to forgive, even though her sins against him were unintentional?

When the seeds were catalogued and tucked in the crisper in her refrigerator, Frankie felt restless. She couldn't spend another day sitting around waiting for her cell phone to ring. Maybe a drive would help.

She took her usual route along Cleveland Avenue past the hardware store, shooting glances into every alley in the hope of spotting the little red wagon. From there she drove across the railroad tracks to Akron Street and pulled in the entrance of Madison Park. It seemed to her that more tents had sprung up since she'd been here last. Was one of them Lilly's?

Please let me find her.

It became a heartsong pulsing in her ears as she walked along the bike path, staring at each tent.

Let me find her. Let me find Lilly.

She watched the tent people going about their lives with great sadness; people sleeping under trees, or hanging laundry from low branches, children playing in the tall weeds along the tracks, each one of them involved in their own storm. But what could she do to help them? She was only one person.

God, what should I do?

The answer came softly, quietly. It told her the common sense solution to people's basic needs was food, clothing and shelter. She couldn't give them all shelter, but she could certainly provide lunch. She returned to her car and checked her wallet. She had fifty-three dollars. It wasn't much, but it was a start.

She drove to a nearby pizzeria and ordered two sheet pizzas, then went across the street to a mini mart and bought a case of bottled water, a package of napkins, and two bright red kick balls.

Forty minutes later she returned to the park. Heart pounding, she carried the pizzas to a picnic table near the tents and sat down. She opened a pizza box, took out a slice, and ate it slowly. It stuck in her throat like concrete. She could feel eyes staring at her from under trees and from inside tents.

Let me not offend them, God. Let me see them the way you do...

The first person to approach her was a little boy. He inched closer to the table, watching her eat with his large, solemn eyes.

"Hi!" she said.

He didn't answer, only inched closer.

"My name's Frankie. What's yours?"

"I like pizza."

"You do?"

He nodded.

"Well I have a lot of it here. Why don't you go and ask your mother if you can have a slice?"

He turned and tore across the park, disappearing into a tent. Moments later a woman marched toward her with the boy and two other children in tow.

"Jade said you was gonna give him some pizza," she said, almost accusingly.

"That's right."

"Be all right if my other kids have some, too?"

"Help yourself. There's bottled water, too."

The woman sat. She was not much more than a girl, really, maybe nineteen or twenty years old. Her pleasure was almost palpable as she sank her teeth into a slice of pepperoni pizza.

Noticing Frankie watching her, she asked, "Why are you doing this?"

Frankie smiled and shrugged. "Why not?"

She found out the girl's name was Junelle. Her boyfriend, Tray, had been laid off from his factory job months before and had gone to Columbus in search of work. She hadn't seen him since.

Others came then, too. They came humbly and suspiciously, thankfully, and with arrogance, and Frankie offered them pizza and a chance to tell her their stories. They talked about deaths, lost jobs, drugs and abuse. They talked, even when the last crumb of pizza and the last bottle of water had been consumed. And talking with them, she realized that more than food, more than clothing and shelter and jobs, people needed to speak, and to be heard. To be spoken to like people, and not like homeless people.

And for the first time in her life, Frankie got it. It was not about trying to save the world. It was about loving people the best you can, one person at a time.

She'd sat in church every Sunday of her life, and on Monday she'd seen the down-and-out holding signs under bridges and beside abandoned factories. And she'd turned her eyes away, thinking the problem was too big, that there was nothing she could do.

Forgive me. Please forgive me…

As the sun began to set she drove home, knowing that today, in each hungry face, she had seen the face of God.

Back home she remembered she'd set her phone on vibrate. She pulled it out of her purse and saw she had a missed text message. She clicked the envelope and read the message. Then sucked in a breath and read it again.

Ur friend is living at Funland. Under the roller coaster.

Chapter Twenty-three

Frankie awoke the next morning feeling as though her head was full of cotton. She poured a cup of coffee and drank it black. The stronger the better, she thought. She'd barely slept the night before.

Her first impulse after reading the text message was to get back in the car and head to Funland. But she knew that was crazy. By then it was dark out, and she didn't even know where Funland was.

A search of the Internet told her the abandoned amusement park was located on Port Arthur's East Side, just outside the city limits, at the end of Portsmouth Avenue.

She wasn't familiar with the east side of town, but Port Arthur was not that big and she was sure she could find it. A further search uncovered a local ghost hunting crew's photo documentary on the old amusement park.

Frankie didn't go in for ghosts and goblins, but the photos showed her exactly what she needed to know. The roller coaster was at the far left side of the park, between the Ferris wheel the Fun House.

A gut feeling told her that the text message couldn't have come from anyone but Scat. If Scat knew that Lilly was living at Funland, it was likely that he was living there, too. Maybe she could find them both. Maybe this was her chance to make things right.

Those were the thoughts that kept her lying awake late into the night. But the morning light made things more clear, and she knew that she'd have to tread carefully. She'd think about it for a day, maybe two, and then decide the best course of action.

It was an unseasonably warm morning, so she dressed in a pair of capris and a lightweight blouse. An ominous heat enveloped her as she walked out the back door.

She cast an anxious glance at the sky. Why was it so dark out? It was nearly eight o'clock. The hot air enveloped her like a wool coat. She could already feel her blouse sticking to her back.

She arrived at school and set about prepping for the day's meal; one of Chelsea's garden veggie salads and her own Italian Wedding soup. Removing a package of pork from the cooler, she added bread crumbs and Parmesan cheese and began forming the mixture into meatballs.

The family recipe soups she served the students once a week had become her most popular lunches. The older girls, who were perpetually dieting, liked the soups because they were low in calories. The boys just liked the flavor. Even Chelsea couldn't find fault with Frankie's soups.

When the students began to arrive, she served them their lunches, keeping an eye on the sky outside the cafeteria window. By noon fat drops of rain began to fall and the wind was bending the old pine trees that surrounded the building. She had just served the last round of lunches when Chelsea appeared in her office.

Since the day Frankie had put her in her place, the woman had been almost pleasant. She seemed to understand now that Frankie could be pushed just so far, and not a bit farther.

"Hey, just a heads up," she said, "you'll want to finish up in here as quickly as you can today. We're closing school at one o'clock."

"We are? Why?"

"Because we have a major storm system rolling in. Haven't you been following the weather reports?"

"Actually, I haven't."

"Well, you should turn on the radio. From what they're saying it's going to be a pretty wild ride."

When Chelsea left, Frankie turned on the small radio above the sink and listened to the news while she washed the dishes. As she listened, the broadcast was interrupted by a series of high-pitched beeps.

"The National Weather Service has issued a severe storm warning for all of Dagon County, Ohio and Pace County, West Virginia. The warning is in effect from two PM until six PM," the automated voice informed her. "The storm system will bring winds of up to sixty miles per hour. Heavy rains may cause flash flooding. All Dagon County, Ohio and Pace County, West Virginia residents are strongly advised to seek shelter. Repeat. The National Weather Service has issued a severe—"

The report made her uneasy and she switched the radio off. She stacked the clean dishes in the racks and wiped down the counters, her stomach aching with dread. She had a nice, dry basement to retreat to if need be. Where would Lilly go to find shelter?

She heard a sharp rapping sound and looked up as a tree branch smacked against the window. Looking out, she saw that the sky was now slate gray. A cascade of shingles had been torn loose from the roof. They cartwheeled across the schoolyard. It was getting rough out there. She wouldn't be able to wait until tomorrow, after all. She would have to go and find Lilly today.

At one fifteen, after the last of the parents had come to collect their children, Frankie got in her car and headed to Portsmouth Avenue.

•

He'd just wanted to make sure she was all right.

The radio had reported that all of the local schools were closing early due to the oncoming storm, so he'd driven by Frankie's house, wanting to see if she'd gotten home safely. Not finding her there, he drove by Holy Child just as her car was pulling out of the lot. Instead of heading toward home, though, like he expected her to, she turned east.

He thought maybe she was going to the store for milk and bread and such, but it soon became obvious she was leaving the leaving city limits.

As if on schedule, the rain went from a drizzle to a downpour and now he was having trouble keeping her in his sites. Where on earth was she going?

It wasn't the first time he'd followed her. Since the altercation with Dalton at the old hardware store, he'd driven by her house almost every night. And twice he'd followed behind her car, like a love- sick teenager. Or a psychopath. He felt the need to be near her, even if she didn't know he was there.

After another half mile she turned onto Portsmouth Avenue, continuing for several blocks. He peered through the rain at her taillights. There were no stores and very few houses at the east end of Portsmouth. The only thing out there was the old amusement park. Surely she wasn't going there?

Funland Amusement Park, like the Foxfire Theater, had opened in the 1920s, in Port Arthur's heyday. For five decades the amusement park had enjoyed huge popularity as a family entertainment venue, with rides, shuffleboard, roller skating, and its trademark fried chicken dinners. The park eventually fell on hard financial times and closed in the 1970s.

Unlike the theater, it never reopened. These days it was a breeding ground for prostitution and drug activity. It was outside of the city limits, so the cops mostly left it alone.

The car directly in front of him stalled, slowing him down. Muttering under his breath, he eased the truck around it. By the time he pulled into the lot at Funland, Frankie's car was already parked and empty. Squinting through the rain, he could see a figure running at the edge of the overgrown lot. Frankie.

What on earth was she thinking?

He scrambled from his truck and cupped his hands around his mouth.

"Frankie!"

For a moment she stopped and looked back. Then she turned and kept going.

Tracy had been to the park only once before, on a dare, when he was a teenager. His challenge had been to retrieve a souvenir from the old roller coaster. The light bulb he'd stolen had earned him his five minutes of fame: two weeks of being the cool guy at his high school.

He'd been nonchalant about it, but in truth, climbing the rickety old roller coaster had scared him half to death. It looked like that was where Frankie was heading now. But why? For God's sake, why?

Racing after her, he gave it all he had, doubled against the wind, deflecting pieces of flying debris with his arms. As he turned a corner in the weedy path, he saw Frankie entering a cardboard lean-to beneath the roller coaster. Thirty-five years had not improved the structure's stability. It swayed like a drunken white monster in the wind, looking as though it could collapse at any moment.

"Oh my God," he whispered.

With a tearing crash, the sign above the roller broke loose, raining debris down on the ground beneath it and puncturing the cardboard roof.

"Frankie!"

As he raced forward, she emerged from the lean-to. Even from a distance, he could see she'd been struck. The right side of her face was covered in blood. She took a step forward, staggered, and fell to the ground.

When he reached her side, she was unconscious, rain mixing with the blood that poured from her wound. So much blood. He had to stop the flow somehow. Somehow.

Oh, Frankie. Please, God… Please.

Carefully, oh so carefully, supporting her head, he lifted her. Shielding her body from the rain with his, he carried her, struggling against the rain and the furious, wailing wind, to the only shelter available. The door to the Fun House was jammed shut. With a ferocious kick, he shattered it and carried her inside.

Laying her gently on the floor, he stripped off his tee shirt. He had to stop the bleeding, somehow.

Please, God…

He tore his shirt into two pieces, doubled them. Frankie's eyes opened.

"Tracy?" A whisper, as if talking was too much effort.

He forced himself to be calm, for her sake. "Hello, sweetheart."

"I'm sorry."

He pressed one of the makeshift bandages to her eye, then tore a strip from the other half of his shirt, all the while, forcing himself to stay calm, for Frankie's sake.

"What were you doing out there?" he asked.

"I was trying to … find my … friend."

He tore another strip, wound it tight over the bandage. The blood kept pouring through. He would need more fabric. "Tracy, I can't see out of my eye."

"I know. It'll be all right."

He tore the last of his shirt into strips. "I'm going to have to cover both of your eyes, Frankie. It's the only way to keep the bandages in place. You won't be able to see anything for a while. But I'll be right here, okay?"

"Okay."

He secured the bandage with the last of his shirt. It wasn't enough. The blood seeped through almost immediately. *God… Please.*

"I need more cloth." He looked around wildly, desperately.

"Here. Use mine."

As if Tracy was having a strange and vivid dream, Dalton was there. Dalton, pulling off his shirt, holding it out like a white flag. Dalton.

"Thank you."

He tore the shirt into strips, padding the first bandage, applying pressure.

"Is she going to be okay?"

"I don't know. I hope so. Here, press on this."

Dalton placed his hands on the bandages while Tracy pulled out his cell phone.

"Yeah, we're out at the old amusement park on Portsmouth Avenue. My friend has been hit by some falling debris. She's bleeding pretty badly."

"I don't know how soon I can get anyone out there. We've got squads out all over the city and a lot of the streets are impassable with flooding. Is she conscious?"

He grabbed her hand, squeezed. She squeezed back "Yes."

"It might have to wait until the rain lets up, unless you want to try and bring her in yourself?"

He glanced out at the pounding rain. Driving in that kind of water would be suicide. He'd have to wait until the rain let up. He only hoped that by then it wouldn't be too late.

He sat, cradling her like a child, Dalton holding her hand, and waited. He kept talking, talking, trying to keep her awake. As long as she was awake, she was all right.

He talked about different storms he'd been through, and the years he'd seen the Ohio River flood. The year it reached as high as the door knobs of the businesses on Main Street. He talked about movies he'd seen, books he'd read, songs he'd heard, anything to keep talking. Anything to keep Frankie awake.

The Fun House roof began to leak, and water poured in, turning the dirt floor to mud around them, and still, Tracy talked.

And when Tracy could think of nothing more to talk about, Dalton took over. He talked about amusement parks and family vacations and the time Tracy had taken him to the Ohio State Fair in Columbus.

"Just picture it, Ms. Bonetti. Me and my girlfriend and my dad at a Ted Nugent concert."

Frankie smiled, and for that, Tracy would be ever grateful to his son.

"Do you remember the summer we went to that amusement park in New York?"

"Lake George," Tracy said. Good Lord. He hadn't thought of that in years.

"We went to that park, Story Town or some such place, and they had that ginormous statue of Davy Crocket?"

"It was Paul Bunyan," Tracy said.

"Right. I was terrified of that thing."

"I remember that. Your mother wanted your picture by that statue so badly, but we couldn't get you to stop crying."

"Of course I couldn't stop crying. A hundred foot tall statue and dude's got a hatchet in his hand that's, like, bigger than me. Who thought that was a good idea?"

"Your mother, probably."

Frankie laughed softly against his chest. He kissed the top of her head. "How are you holding up? You doing okay?"

"I think so."

He hitched her closer, wanting it to be true.

"And then there was that time I got lost in that wax museum

and I got rescued by Frankenstein. Remember, I screamed so loud the security guard thought someone was being murdered?"

"Don't you have any good memories of your childhood?" Tracy asked.

"Yeah," Dalton said softly. "I do."

•

After nearly two hours, the downpour slowed to a drizzle.

"Frankie?"

"Yes?"

"It looks like the rain is letting up. I'm going to try and take you to the hospital now."

"Okay."

Setting her gently in Dalton's arms, Tracy stood to his feet, working the cramps from his legs. When he was sure he could walk, he squatted and lifted her in his arms.

Dalton stood. "Dad? Is it all right if I go with you?"

Chapter Twenty-four

The emergency room at William Cloud Memorial Hospital was normally a loud, chaotic mess of accident victims, drug overdoses, and cases of the flu. Tonight the pandemonium was made worse by people struck by flying debris, or injured by collapsed roofs.

It had taken Tracy an hour and a half to get across town. Inch by inch, he'd propelled his truck through the flooded streets, through an obstacle course of fallen trees and downed power lines, houses and buildings up to their windows in water. He'd seen Port Arthur this way before, but even so, the flooding never failed to horrify him.

He found a wheelchair in the Emergency Room's front entrance and gently set Frankie down in it, then wheeled her to the registration desk. He gave the on-duty nurse her information and the insurance card he'd found in her purse.

"She'll have to sit in the waiting area until a doctor is free. It's probably going to be awhile."

As he glanced into the mobbed waiting room, his heart sank. "Please. She's lost a lot of blood."

The nurse glanced at the blood-stained bandages around Frankie's eyes. She sighed. "All right. I'll see if the next available doctor will treat her." As Tracy wheeled her around the desk, the nurse's hand shot out. "Wait, hold it. You two can't come in here like that."

Tracy looked down at his bare, mud-caked chest, and then at Dalton's. "We used our shirts to stop her bleeding."

The nurse sighed again. "Hang on."

She retreated to a small room behind the desk and returned

with two paper exam gowns, which she handed to Tracy. "You can put these on for now."

Donning the paper gowns, they wheeled Frankie into the waiting room.

"It shouldn't be too long now," Tracy told her. "You still doing okay?"

"It hurts."

He gently massaged the base of her neck. "I know, sweetheart. Try to hold on."

She turned her face in Dalton's direction. "Scat, do you know where Lilly is?"

"I'm sorry, Ms. Bonetti. I don't know."

After an excruciatingly long wait, a nurse came and wheeled Frankie into an exam room. Tracy sank back in his chair, overtaken by exhaustion. He massaged his cat-scratched eyes.

"Hey, Dad?" Dalton said quietly. 'I just want to say I'm sorry. About everything."

He opened his eyes and regarded his son. "I'm the one who's sorry, Dalton. A sorry excuse for a father. Allie explained to me about the rehab center in Florida, and why you came back to Port Arthur. I didn't understand. I didn't even try."

"I should have come to you right away. As soon as I got home."

"I'm sorry you didn't feel you could."

"I shouldn't have stolen from the company in the first place. I let you down. I let mom down."

"Your mother loved you more than life. I guess after losing her we both kind of came apart."

"Yeah," he said softly. Then, "Ms. Bonetti … I mean Frankie. She reminds me a lot of mom. She's, you know, gentle like mom was."

"I know."

"You should hold on to her."

Count on it, Son, he thought.

"Those memories you shared today, about your childhood… I'd like it if we could make some more of them." He stared at his hands. "I hope it's not too late."

"I'd like that, too," Dalton said, his voice cracking.

And then Tracy did what he'd wanted to do for two solid years. He wrapped his arms around his son and pulled him to his chest. "You're my son," he said softly. "You'll always be my son. No matter what happens."

A sob caught in Dalton's throat. "Thanks."

For an eternity, they waited, each lost in his own thoughts. Tracy found himself praying as he hadn't prayed in years.

Let her be all right. Gracious Lord, Please give me another chance...

It was nearly nine o'clock when the on-duty nurse called his name. He hurried to the desk with Dalton right behind him.

"She'll be out shortly," she told them.

"How is she?"

"Doctor Harris is the one that treated her. He'll come out and talk with you."

A short time later a man in a rumpled pair of scrubs appeared at the desk, looking much too young to be a doctor. He looked as tired as Tracy felt.

"Are you Tracy Johanson?" he asked.

"Yes."

"We sent her for x-rays, that's what took so long. The worst of it is a concussion and a broken nose. Though if you hadn't gotten the bleeding under control, she probably wouldn't have made it.

We've cleaned the wound and stitched it up. That's all we can do here in the ER. Once the swelling goes down, she should probably see an ophthalmologist, just to make sure there's no nerve damage to the eye. I'd like to keep her overnight, but to be honest we don't have an empty bed."

"I'll take her home and keep an eye on her."

"We've started her on an antibiotic and given her something for pain. You can fill these tomorrow." He gave Tracy prescriptions for pain medicine and antibiotics and then they brought Frankie out. Her face was bruised and swollen and she was splattered with mud from head to toe. Tracy thought she had never looked more beautiful.

•

Back home, he helped her to the bathroom.

"There's a box of your mother's things down in the cellar," he told Dalton. "Go and see if you can find her something dry to put on."

He ran a sink full of warm water and washed the dirt from Frankie's arms and legs the best he could. Dalton returned with a flannel night gown and Tracy eased it over her head. In the living room, he settled her on the couch with blankets and pillows.

"All right if I go and take a shower?" Dalton asked. Tracy regarded his son's paper gown and mud-caked pants. "Please do. And then go and get some sleep."

He lingered for a moment. "Are you sure?"

"Dalton, go. I've got this."

As Dalton went gratefully off to shower, Tracy carefully stretched out on the couch beside Frankie.

"It's been quite a day," he said. "Hasn't it?"

"They said you saved my life."

He shrugged. "I just made a couple of bandages."

"What made you follow me today?"

"I was only going to make sure you got home from school all right. When I saw you heading out of town, I got worried."

"I'm sure glad you did."

"You're a crazy, stubborn, beautiful woman, Frankie Bonetti."

"And you're a crazy, stubborn, beautiful man."

He gently put his arm around her, tearing the paper gown. He ripped it off and threw it across the room, and they laughed softly. And then the day finally caught up with him; the terrible, wonderful, gut-twisting, heart-wrenching day. Tears gathered on his lashes. "I didn't want to lose you." He kissed her forehead, and then her lips. "I don't ever want to lose you."

She smiled, her eyelids heavy.

"I've acted like a fool for the past couple of weeks. Can you forgive me?"

"I already have."

"I realized today how easily the things you love can be lost. It's a lesson I should have learned a long time ago."

She snuggled closer against his chest. "Mhmmm."

Rain began to fall again, beating a rhythm against the windows. Lying there, with Frankie safe in his arms, he thanked God for second chances. He prayed for strength to be a better man, for both her and for Dalton. Mostly, he prayed for courage. Because he knew what he wanted now. And he hoped she wanted the same thing.

Closing his eyes, he pushed the words out. "I love you, Frankie. I have for a long time now. What I'm trying to say, what I've wanted to say for a very long time is, I want to marry you. If you'll have me."

He expected a flat out refusal. Or a tearful acceptance. What he didn't expect was silence. Opening his eyes, he chanced a glance at her face. Then he smiled. She was fast asleep.

Chapter Twenty-five

It was two weeks before Port Arthur returned to something that resembled normal. After ten days, the water receded. After twelve, the power lines were restored. After thirteen, the streets and businesses reopened. Basements were pumped and roofs were repaired. And Frankie returned to work.

She'd stayed with Tracy for three days, with Rhoda and Allie camped out in the living room, fussing over her every move. After a week, most of the swelling in her face had gone down, leaving a raccoon mask of purple bruises around her eyes and nose.

She'd received a good report from the ophthalmologist; there was no permanent damage to her eye. She was left with an angry, two-inch scar that ran from her hairline to the corner of her right eye.

The scar would fade with time, she was told, but it would never completely go away. Frankie didn't care. She was more alive, and more in love than ever before in her life. She felt beautiful on the inside. And that was all that mattered.

Driving to work for the first time since the storm, she saw that several of the decrepit buildings on Cleveland Avenue, among them the old hardware store, had finally collapsed. Good riddance, she thought. She only hoped no one had been hurt.

She walked through the front door of Holy Child Academy to find Tony Argentari waiting for her.

"It's good to have you back, Frankie."

"Thank you, Tony."

"If the day gets to be too much for you, don't feel you have to stay. We're keeping the temp for another week to help you out."

"I appreciate that."

Chelsea was banging around in the kitchen when she walked in.

"Boy am I glad to see you!" she said.

Smiling, Frankie gazed around at the menagerie of pots and pans and kitchen gadgets that were strewn across the counters. "What are you doing?"

"I've been coming in early every day to start the prep work. This temp Tony hired doesn't do a thing, and it takes her all darn day to do it. The woman can't even manage to boil water."

"Oh, dear."

Chelsea smiled. "Seriously, Frankie. I'm glad you're back. We were pretty worried about you."

Madeline Simms, the woman from the temporary agency, was a retired restaurant owner and a compulsive chatterer. It didn't take long for Frankie to see why she and Chelsea hadn't hit it off.

The woman could not seem to work and talk at the same time, but the students loved her. She took the time to speak to each child that came through the lunch line, and Frankie was amazed that she'd already learned all of their names.

But it was Frankie they sought out, Frankie they brought cards and bouquets of autumn leaves and bags of Hershey's kisses to. She ended her first day back at work feeling satisfied, but exhausted. She'd taken to napping in the afternoons ever since the accident. She drove home, longing for an hour or two of sleep. She'd get up and shower before Tracy arrived, sleeping only long enough to feel human again.

When her house came into view, she slowed the car and gave it a hard glance. It looked like someone was sitting on her porch.

Drawing closer, she cried out softly. "Oh, thank God."

Barreling into the driveway, she flung herself from the car and raced around to the front of the house.

"Lilly?"

Her friend stood, smiling uncertainly. "How are you doing, girl?"

"Oh, thank God." Frankie flung herself at her friend and gathered her into a hug. "Oh, thank you, Jesus. You're safe."

Lilly held her at arm's length and studied her face. "Lord have mercy, if you don't look just like one of them roller derby queens."

Frankie laughed, and then burst into tears. "I have been so worried about you."

"Hey, now. You don't need to shed no tears on my account, Frankie Bonetti. I been just fine."

Frankie held her for another long moment, savoring the miracle of it. Lilly. Right here, on her front porch. "Let's go inside," she said. "I have biscotti. "

The cats couldn't stop purring, couldn't stop rubbing around Lilly's ankles. She picked Nutmeg up and scratched him under the chin. "How's my boys, huh? Did you miss me?"

He sat in her lap, kneading her skirt with his paws. Frankie set a plate of biscotti on the table in front of Lilly and poured two glasses of iced cider.

"Tell me everything," she said. "Where have you been all this time?"

"The city opened up a temporary shelter in the old Episcopalian church on Chillicothe Street. I've been staying there ever since the storm."

"Good. That's good. Is it a nice place?"

"It ain't what you'd call the Ritz," she shrugged. "It's okay." She picked up a cookie, then set it back down, her gaze traveling to her hands.

"What is it, Lilly?"

"You come out there looking for me didn't you? Out to Funland on the day of the storm?"

"How do you know about that?

"I was there in the Fun House that day. Hiding in the back. I didn't say anything. I was too ashamed. I was afraid your man would give me the tongue lashing I deserved." Tears sprang to her eyes. "I've been a foolish old woman, and I treated you just horrible. I'm so sorry, Frankie."

"No, Lilly. I'm sorry. I'm sorry I tried to force you into something you weren't comfortable with. I hurt your feelings and your pride. I should never have done that."

"You was only being you. Saint Frankie of Assisi."

Frankie smiled.

"The reason I sent you away that day, it wasn't about you at all. It was about me and all the stupid choices I made. I couldn't come here and live with you, because I don't deserve to. I deserve everything I got in life."

Frankie's smile faded. "No one deserves to be homeless."

"I do."

"What would make you think such a thing?"

"You'll hate me if I tell you."

"No I won't. I promise."

She stared at her hands again for a long moment, gathering her thoughts. Finally she said, "Growing up, we had it hard, my family. There was money, but never enough for any extras. Daddy's nursery put food on our table and kept the lights on and not much else. We were happy though, mostly, my sisters and me. We had mom and daddy, and each other. And flowers. We couldn't think of nothing else we wanted.

"Then I become a teenager. I looked around and I saw everything I didn't have. And then I wasn't happy no more. I met Harvey one night at a fire hall dance. He was twenty six, ten years older than me. Oh, I thought that man was fine. He had a good job in the metal factory and he made good money, and the best part was that he wanted to spend some of it on me. For the first time in my life I had nice clothes and jewelry and perfume that didn't come from Woolworth's. I wanted those things, Frankie. I wanted 'em more than anything."

"Every young girl does," Frankie said.

"Maybe so. But not every young girl would do what I done."

She hesitated and Frankie waited.

"I knew Harvey was married. I knew it and I didn't care. Two months after I met him I let myself get pregnant. I just wanted to try and hold on to him any way I could. Harvey, he left his wife and married me.

"My daddy begged me not to marry him. He said Harvey had a mean streak as wide as the sky, and that he drank too much. He said him and mom would help me raise the baby but I didn't listen. I didn't listen to my daddy and I got exactly what

I deserved. Twenty seven years of misery and beatings. My kids, my beautiful kids, abused and degraded. They left home soon's they could, and they never looked back. Then Harvey died. I hated him, but life was worse without him, some ways. The poverty, I mean. I couldn't hold onto my house. I didn't know how to support myself. I'd never had to before. In the end I lost everything. Didn't care about possessions so much, but I do miss them kids something fierce. That's the price I paid for stealing another woman's husband."

"Oh, Lilly." She reached across the table and held Lilly's hand. "We all make poor choices sometimes."

"Not you."

"Yes, me. I married a man I didn't love just so I wouldn't be alone. And then I ended up more alone than ever. I didn't wait for God to send the right man. Maybe I didn't trust him to. But one thing I know for sure, and that's that God forgives anyone who is truly sorry. The hard part is learning to forgive ourselves."

"You're the best friend I ever had, Frankie Bonetti. And way more of a friend than I deserve."

Feeling the time was right, Frankie offered up a silent prayer for wisdom. "Let me ask you a favor then, as a friend."

"Ask it, girl. I'll do it if I can."

"I'm going to need some help around here. Someone to take care of the cats and tidy up the house until I'm a hundred percent again. Would you stay with me for a while? At least through the winter?"

Lilly nodded and placed her free hand on top of Frankie's. "Don't you worry about a thing, honey. I'll stay as long as you need me to."

Epilogue

Coffee in hand, Frankie stepped onto her back deck in the soft May morning. She paused to breathe in the perfumed air. The tulips she and Lilly planted last fall were in full bloom now, making her yard a lovely menagerie of pink and purple, red, gold and orange. Add to that the baskets of mixed flowers Rhoda brought yesterday and tucked into every available space and you had a wonderland.

Padding out to the old barn, she unlocked the door and stepped inside. Closing her eyes, she flipped the light switch. When she opened them again, her breath caught. She gazed in wonder at a room she barely recognized.

Everywhere she looked, white lights twinkled. They hung from the ceiling beams and cascaded down the walls and wound their way softly through the branches of a dozen pink hibiscus trees. In the center of the room, where the buffet tables had been, there were now small, cozy round tables dressed in white linen cloths, vases of palest pink hydrangeas and matching pillar candles gracing the center of every one. Setting down her coffee, she hugged herself.

"I love this," she whispered.

"Ooh, girl, what are you doing out here? You wasn't supposed to see this yet."

"Lilly, this looks amazing."

"It does, don't it." Lilly beamed. "Allie and Scat done most of it, after Rhoda drew it all out for us. For once I was happy that woman took control. "

"I love the lights. I think we should leave them up, afterwards, don't you?"

"Definitely."

"We'll open up the big doors later and have the dancing in the driveway."

"That's the plan. Now don't you fret yourself about any of the small stuff."

"I won't."

"It's gonna be a beautiful reception, Frankie. It all come together just perfect."

She smiled. "It did, didn't it?"

Over the long winter, Tracy had worked to restore the old barn. He'd gutted the inside and put on a new roof. He'd overhauled the wiring, installed sinks and ovens in the back, and added plenty of shelving out front. They'd bought buffet tables and metal folding chairs. And on April first, Frankie's Heart Food Pantry and Soup Kitchen served its first official meal.

Scat had written articles for the Port Arthur papers and sent them along to newspapers in Cincinnati and Columbus, and donations had started pouring in. It restored Frankie's faith in human goodness.

People wanted to help, she realized. They just didn't know what to do. Now she and Lilly served fifty meals on an average Saturday, and gave away more than a hundred pounds of food and hygiene products every week. But for today, the barn was her own. A wonderful wedding wonderland.

"I do wish we'd ordered more than one Port-A-Potty," Lilly fretted. "We got sixty-five people coming. Half of 'em gonna end using the bathroom inside. Even if they are family, that's an awful lotta people messin' up your house."

"It's your house now, Lilly."

"Exactly."

•

It was just as she'd always dreamed it would be, and yet it was like nothing she'd ever imagined.

The pews at St. Bridgette's overflowed with people, its altar with flowers, and all around her, Frankie felt the presence of love. It radiated from the ceiling and the walls, and from the old pipe organ. From Rhoda, in her pale pink gown, and from

Lilly, in her burgundy one.

From Scat and Guy, dashing in their gray tuxedos.

From Sal as he tucked her hand into the crook of his arm. "Looks like it's time."

She pushed out a breath. "Wow. Okay."

"You look stunning, Frankie."

And in her white lace gown, with pink roses in her hair, despite her scar, she felt that it was true. She was beautiful, not because of all these things, but because she was loved.

"You got this," Rhoda whispered. Planting a quick kiss on Frankie's cheek, she headed down the aisle.

"Here goes nothing." Lilly squeezed her hand, and then she, too made her way to the front, wobbling in her high heels. From where she stood, she could see Tracy at the altar, waiting for her, and she knew without a doubt that this was the moment she'd waited her whole life for.

Her eyes rested for a moment on the statue of the Good Shepherd. A gentle hush came over her, and she was like the little lamb cradled in his arms, utterly cherished by the Shepherd, unspeakably loved.

Thank You, God. For rivers in the desert. For this man, and this moment, and for new beginnings.

And then, three hundred and sixty-five days after the day she first opened her door to Tracy Johanson, Frankie opened her heart up wide. As the wedding march began, she took her first step toward the altar, leaving her old life behind, ready for her new life to begin.

The End